T0349416

DIABLO®

Shadows of Sanctuary

A SHORT STORY COLLECTION

DIABLO®

Shadows of Sanctuary

A SHORT STORY COLLECTION

Z BREWER • ALMA KATSU
JONATHAN MABERRY • RYAN QUINN
CARLY ANNE WEST

BLIZZARD ENTERTAINMENT

Published by Blizzard Entertainment.

Library of Congress Cataloging-in-Publication Data available.

ISBN: 978-1-956916-64-5

Manufactured in China

Print run 10 9 8 7 6 5 4 3 2 1

Contents

WITNESS • 9
ALMA KATSU

SANCTUM OF BONE • 51
CARLY ANNE WEST

TEETH OF THE PLAGUE • 91
Z BREWER

THE TOLL OF DARKNESS AND LIGHT • 117
JONATHAN MABERRY

INSTINCTS • 149
RYAN QUINN

WE ARE ALL GUILTY • 193
RYAN QUINN

Witness

A SHORT STORY BY

ALMA KATSU

WITNESS

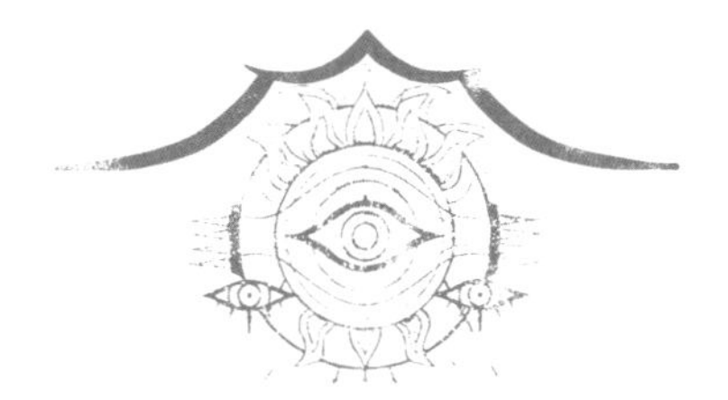

I always know when a visitor is about to arrive. The air in my parlor—normally still and close with woodsmoke and dust—shimmers like it is alive.

And shortly, it *is*.

Within minutes, a stranger materializes, becomes flesh and blood out of the nothingness in front of me.

First-time visitors are inevitably surprised, suddenly finding themselves in an unfamiliar parlor, facing a mysterious figure shrouded in shadow and fog. Is it what they expected? Sometimes they have been sent against their will and have no idea what is happening to them. But usually they choose to make this journey, even if they don't know that it will take them here. I don't know what they have been told to expect, and I never ask them.

I must keep my distance from these visitors. I am a scribe. A diligent recorder of history. To ask would go against the rules.

But I am something else too. I am a facilitator in the affairs of mortals.

I watch the air thicken in front of me as it pushes into another dimension. Colors appear: the gray haze of smoke, blinding slivers of white, nuggets of the man's blue eyes, the glint of the metal hilt of his sword. Then he is standing whole, in front of me. This one is tall and thin and wiry. His age is elusive—not young, not old—but he is clearly strong and nimble. His hair is long, but his face doesn't match the number of years it takes to become that silver-gray. He wears traveler's clothes, a cloak and good boots, all well made and costly but showing the miles. He takes off his broad-brimmed hat to reveal a foxlike face. High cheekbones, a pointy nose. There is intelligence in those eyes but also a touch of frost: his guard is up. Far and away, the most honest of his features is his mouth, which is wry and cunning and tight.

There's something about this one. And it is not just his sword. It is a serious blade, meant for use. Not merely a warning.

He isn't disoriented for long, not like most visitors. Sometimes guests come through their dreams, but most often they make the journey from Sanctuary using elixirs and even certain teas. He seems to be recovering from the effects quickly. He likely didn't take much of whatever he took, or perhaps he used the least potent. Not tincture of nightshade or salvia divinorum. Maybe, at worst, a thimble of hound's blood or powdered stag's horn. But it's impossible to know; many of those who claim to be magicians are charlatans, and who knows what they put in their potions?

He closes his eyes and takes a deep breath to steady himself. When he opens those eyes again, his gaze settles on me. My hair is still mostly black, my eyes a watery sea green. If someone were to come in search of a Damji, to look at me they would know they had found one.

Regardless, my clothing has been chosen to conceal. There is little exposed skin between my leggings, sleeves, and a bodice formed of leather straps and bronze fittings. A hood conceals the particulars of my face, hides too the telltale eye darts and flickers that could reveal what I am thinking. I cannot let visitors know what is really going on in my mind. The hood lets the visitor see what will comfort them and draw them in: my striking pale eyes and the smile that many tell me is bewitching still. A smile meant to put a visitor at ease, promising a patient, sympathetic ear.

His gaze drops to my hands and forearms. Tattoos peek out from my sleeves. They could be mistaken for symbols, but they are words. He won't be able to discern their meaning. The language is dead and long gone. But over the words are new images, drawings that crawl over the old tattoos, that curl around them, meld with them, obscure them. My present hiding my past—there's a message there, if one is patient. But his eye

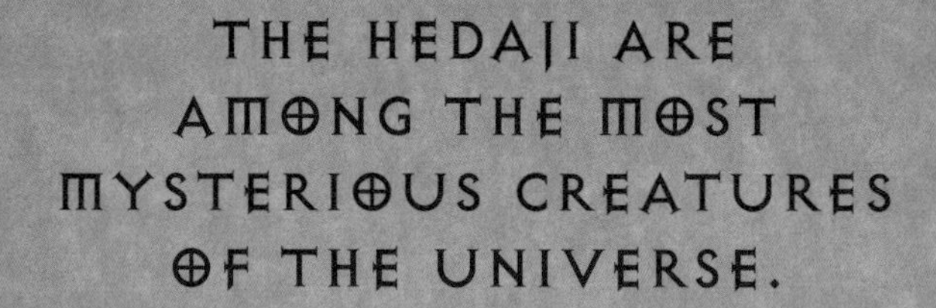

THE HEDAJI ARE
AMONG THE MOST
MYSTERIOUS CREATURES
OF THE UNIVERSE.

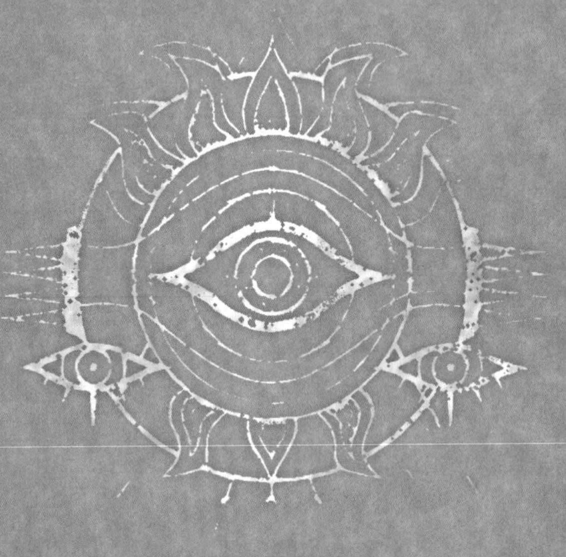

SOME VISITORS
SEEK ME MERELY
OUT OF CURIOSITY.

skitters off quickly and goes down to my ink-stained hands. The stains reach up to the middle of my forearms, for they are a sign of my trade and I have been at it for a long, long time.

He stares at one finger in particular. It's been amputated above the second knuckle and capped with an obscure piece of jewelry: an inkwell. The inkwell is one of the tools of my work. It is the reservoir that holds the dye that mixes with my blood to create a special ink.

He opens his mouth as though he's about to ask a question. Just as quickly, he licks his lips, smiles wolfishly, but asks nothing. Does he know what that amputation signifies?

I'm not about to ask. I am secure in the knowledge that he can't hurt me, and I sense that he knows this too.

"Welcome, stranger," I say with my customary confidence, though today I do not quite feel it. Usually, I am happy to have a visitor. I look forward to the company, the distraction.

But not this time.

Then he smiles as he starts to understand where he is. Where he has landed. "What in the name of all the hells . . . Well, I'll be damned. It worked, didn't it? You're Hedaji, aren't you?"

The Hedaji are among the most mysterious creatures of the universe. Some visitors seek me merely out of curiosity.

I knew nothing about the Hedaji before I met Badaal, the man who would become my mentor. Badaal saw something in me that made him think I would do well as one of them. At the time, I was not in a position to turn him down.

That happened so long ago, in fact, that I have lost track of the exact number of years. Of course, time is meaningless to Hedaji, as it would be to anyone who can see past and present and future.

The stranger doesn't know that he is lucky to be visiting me. I don't need to be modest: I am one of the most respected of the Hedaji. I have been witness to many, many epic feats, recorded many fearsome battles and many glorious deaths. That is because I have never lost my curiosity. Even after all this time, I am eager to learn more. Knowledge is a strength as powerful as armor. Knowledge is a weapon in and of itself. Some Hedaji are content to be summoned to bear witness to one important moment or another, but I have always thrown myself headlong into the hunt. My thirst is endless, my quest boundless.

But the reason for my quest has changed.

The visitor draws back and starts to pace along the walls of the room, like a wild thing trapped in a pen, trying to find a way out. He takes a few steps in one direction, then turns and strides off in another. A bank of fog rises up suddenly and stops him like a wall, and he stands there, trying to find a way around it, even though he can't see it properly, can't tell if it's solid.

"Where am I?" His voice has a singsong quality to it. It makes him sound gentler than he probably is. But he is trapped, and he knows it.

I extend a hand toward the center of the room, attempting to guide him away from the walls. "Welcome, stranger. Take your ease. What's your name?"

"Giaran. My name is Giaran." It won't be his name the moment we part company, of that I have no doubt.

"You're in my parlor. Did you not mean to come here? This is not an easy place to get to. Few people come here by accident..."

"Yes, I came here on purpose. I went to see a reclusive alchemist. He came well recommended. The last thing I remember is drinking this potion..." A hand flutters to his forehead. He closes his eyes, trying to bear down on a memory that wants to slip away.

Something is different about Giaran. Something feels off. "You're fine. You're exactly where you should be. You are welcome to browse—my dwelling is home to many curiosities, many treasures—but know that our time is limited, and I want to see that you get what you came for. Is there something special you seek?"

He looks me up and down now, as though he's never seen the likes of me before. "You are Hedaji, aren't you? The man who gave me the potion said it would summon a Hedaji..."

"The effect is the other way around," I explain gently. "It has brought you to me." As we speak, I can't get over the feeling there is something familiar about him, even though we haven't met before. After all, I have traveled the length and breadth of Sanctuary. I have seen more tribes and clans than most anyone can lay claim to, except the gods themselves, so I don't let myself be distracted by this odd sense of déjà vu.

"My name is Tejal. Come, sit at my table." A huge wooden table materializes between us at my command. It's draped with an ancient red tablecloth, threadbare in places. It's anchored with touchstones: a ceremonial skull, coins of fortune, a divining blade.

He touches the cloth as though to convince himself that it's real, then staggers to the seat opposite me.

"Laid before you is the bounty of history!" The cards appear out of thin air as I reach for them. They dance above my hands, shuffling themselves. When I extend my arms to my sides, the cards fly, fanning into a circle that floats in the air. The visitor gawks, as well he should: it is clear that each card bristles and thrums with a life of its own, each a portal to its own story. And then as I draw my hands back together, the cards follow, falling into place until they are a stack again. Waiting.

For each card, there is an image on the front, usually the likeness of a person but sometimes an object, and that very person or object also appears over my shoulder in a dim light, like a spirit escaping from another plane.

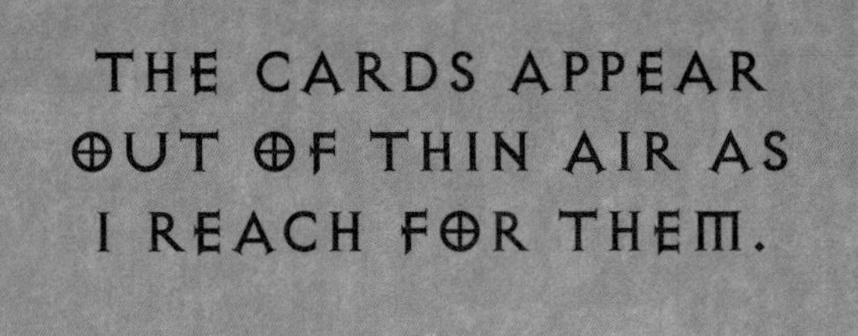

THE CARDS APPEAR
OUT OF THIN AIR AS
I REACH FOR THEM.

THEY DANCE
ABOVE MY HANDS,
SHUFFLING THEMSELVES.

"Perhaps this item is to your liking?" I make the card hover level with Giaran's eyes so he can see the image before flipping the card over to reveal the text, the person's or artifact's story. There's a river of words, tiny and densely packed, too small to read without a glass. Then I flip the card again and the stranger recoils: the image has been replaced by more words as well as a drawing, a study of a detail. An insignia, say, or the exact pattern of scars from a fearsome wound. And on and on it goes as I make the card somersault. The sides keep changing, an endless recounting of the item and the item's owner, an entire book captured on those two small surfaces. The stories inscribed on those cards—I know them by heart. In my humble opinion, that is the true magic of the Hedaji: the infinite amount of wisdom each of us holds. We are worlds within worlds.

The stranger tries to still the card, but it eludes his grasp. "What is this, a trick? What is this you're showing me?"

I ignore his question. He will settle eventually. All visitors are nervous when they first arrive. They will concentrate on the artifacts soon enough, remembering their needs. What brought them here in the first place. "Look carefully." I wave my hand, and we are back at the beginning, at the meticulously rendered illustration of a monstrous rat's skull. It has been thoroughly stripped of fur and flesh, the bone cleaned. The way it has been preserved, it is almost beautiful, and the artwork has captured this, down to the lacquered sheen that has been lovingly applied over bone, the way it adds a veneer of iridescent color over the ivory.

Over my shoulder, the skull appears out of the darkness.

"It was a part of the armor of Vylum, the druidic son of a lord of Westmarch," I tell Giaran. "Have you heard of him? No? He was beloved by the lowly animals of the city's sewers and cellars and mausoleums. Not so beloved by humans." It's not that I think this dapper stranger has come for the scourge of Westmarch's frightening piece; I am merely trying to draw him out. I tap a finger on the image.

"The skull belonged to one of his favorite minions, an intelligent rat by the name of Plato, who was killed by the city guard appointed to exterminate all rats in a time of plague. Plato's master couldn't bear to say goodbye, so he kept his skeleton to adorn his tunic. The Rat King is quite the fearsome sight. Picture him festooned with the bones of his fallen rodent comrades, hides and teeth and tails. He leaves a rat skull as his calling card when he's made a kill, to let his enemies know who was responsible. But he couldn't bear to part with Plato's."

The stranger scowls. Well, it is a disquieting sight, though I sense he is not squeamish. This man is not frightened by the sight of death.

"You know his story well. It's almost like you were there."

"I *was* there." I study his face, hoping for clues to his true desire, but he is like an actor, hiding what he doesn't want me to see.

"That is the Hedaji's role, you know: we travel time and space to record moments of great battle and glory. We are the historians, capturing moments in crystal clarity so they are not lost to time."

I take one last look at the rat's lacquered skull. "Not of interest?" I flick the card away. "Perhaps this is more to your liking?" The rat skull recedes into the darkness, replaced by a huge helmet gray with layers of tarnish.

The stranger leans forward, intrigued by the gilt barely visible beneath the gray. The helmet is, in fact, a massive iron bell that was stripped from a Zakarum church in the little town of Saint's Calling.

"This is the helmet of a barbarian named Klath-Ulna, the Golden One. He was bent on sacking the iron bells from all churches built in the name of the Zakarum faith, and cutting and breaking them into shape to become part of his gold-stamped armor. Sacrilegious, some might say, but Klath-Ulna had long given up on the beliefs of the church. Vengeance became his religion. Besides"—the bell, though molded and carved with a mask of eye sockets and skeletal teeth, still had a lilt of gold that had been grafted onto the bell—"gold brings beauty to this object of terror . . . It mocked his enemies by using that which they idolized to forge his own frightening visage. He made them look into the face of *judgment*."

Giaran licks his lips again as he studies the image. Yes, gold is definitely more to his liking. A man who appreciates coin, then. Perhaps even worships it. Has he come for a piece of Klath-Ulna's legacy? Does the frightening barbarian mean something to him, or is he merely tempted by the presence of so much gold?

He rises from the table and approaches the helmet. It sways heavily in the misty air just beyond his reach.

Then I realize, no, Giaran doesn't want to touch the helmet: he's trying to look *beyond* it. He wasn't confused earlier and trying to find a way out. He's trying to see what other treasures I possess.

Reluctantly, he returns to sit at the table. I flick the card away. The area behind me goes black, and there is nothing else to compete for his attention. It is just him and me.

I decide to confront him directly. "What are you looking for, stranger?"

He turns shy—or maybe obstinate. For a second time, he doesn't answer. He asks, instead, "Are all Hedaji like you?"

"Do you mean, are we related by blood? No, we are more like priests, I suppose: drawn from every clan, every class, every race that exists. I think we're chosen because we possess certain attributes, specific tendencies."

He glances at the spartan walls of the chamber. "You would have to crave solitude, I suppose. It's just you here, in these chambers, isn't it? You're alone."

An icy finger runs down my spine. Should I be worried? Is he probing for weaknesses?

He grins wolfishly again. "It wouldn't be pleasant for someone who needs to be surrounded by people."

When I was a child, people said that I was happiest in the company of others. A born leader, my father had said. He thought I would lead the community of our clan one day, like my mother.

That was not to be, and that girl has been gone for a long time. Though she has been visiting me lately, reminding me of what I once was.

"This lonely life seems to suit you," he says, almost smug. So sure of his judgments, this one. "Does it? Are you happy here, living in the shadows?"

I shuffle the cards. The feel of them in my hands offers a bit of comfort. They are the stories of others. These may not be stories *about* me, but in a way they are my stories too, ones I've recorded over the millennia. They are all I have. They are my children, my family. "It is necessary, regardless of how one may feel personally. We seek out those moments in time that must be captured, the moments that can't afford to be lost."

"I understand you're not allowed to interfere."

"That's right. We are there to record and nothing more. We can't change history, even for the individual."

He leans forward so that our faces are close. I can smell the oil he uses to dress that silvery mane of his and the woodsmoke that clings to his clothing. "But I've heard of a time when a Hedaji did more than just record. When a Hedaji interfered with destiny."

I have the presence of mind not to react. I manage to keep my breathing and my gaze steady. There is no way he could *know*. He is fishing for information. *That* is what he's come here for.

I smirk. "People *want* the Hedaji to break their oath: that would make us seem more human. Relatable. But—no. That is not our way."

He nods. But he is not done yet with this line of questioning. "It must be hard, Tejal, to see all sorts of good people in danger, being killed, and not be able to do something about it."

Is this why he's sought me out? Did I witness some terrible slaughter that is meaningful to him? Has he come for something besides an object? I don't know what that could possibly be.

"It's not my place to become part of the moment. The Hedaji make sure there exists a record. A record is only good if it is shared with others. In that way, the Hedaji fulfill a vital role. We enable remembrance, of both the bad and the good."

He stares at me pointedly: he means to get an answer. He will not put up with my deflections and half-truths any longer. "But surely there have been times when you wanted to take action . . . Debasing of maidens, the slaughter of innocents? Surely you have seen acts so unfair, so unjust, that you knew it was a crime against the universe *not* to act."

He is fired up now, closer to the real reason why he has come here than I have seen yet. Is he here seeking justice? Does he foolishly think I am in a position to give that to him?

Or is he seeking justice *from* me?

"You know little about the universe, friend," is all I can say.

HE IS
SEARCHING

FOR SOMETHING
IN PARTICULAR.

He rises from the table once more and goes into the darkness behind me. He wants to study the pieces I have on display, and this time I allow the shadows to let him go closer. He approaches the shelves, his eye skipping from one object to another. While it makes for an impressive display, my collection is mostly captured in the cards. The physical objects I keep with me are not the most important or most costly.

They are the ones that captured my imagination—or sympathy.

He walks from piece to piece, keeping a respectful distance at all times. He goes slowly, moving on only after he's studied an object with the rapt attention of a scholar. I can't help but think that this is an act, however. He is searching for something in particular.

He doesn't even pause at the scrap of red fabric that's part of my personal collection. Why should he? It's old and tattered and could easily be mistaken for a cleaning rag. He doesn't see the fragment of a faded sigil, barely visible on its corner. The line of a dragon's jaw, the curve of a crescent moon.

He stops at the plainest and most enigmatic piece in my collection. It is a ring, a small thing meant to be worn by a girl or young woman. It's not made of precious metal, has no jewels. It's made of a simple alloy. Affixed to the ring is a long, slender spike about the length of a man's hand. Even though it is a piece of jewelry, this spike has a purpose, and it is not merely adornment.

"This is curious," he says, leaning in for a closer look. "I've never seen anything like it."

"It's very old." I decide to test him. I lift my veil, the better to see him. "It belonged to a clan that's long dead. The Damji. Have you ever heard of them?"

He strokes his chin. "Would you be surprised to hear that I *have*?"

That's impossible.

Who is this man?

His hand hovers over the ring. He looks at me imploringly. "May I?"

I nod, curious to see if, at last, he will reveal himself.

He picks up the artifact, not without reverence. He turns it over, appraising it from every angle. "What is this?"

"What do *you* think?"

He runs a finger down the long end of the spike. "I suppose this could be used as a weapon at close quarters, like a stiletto. You could plunge this end into an assailant's neck . . . or drive it through an eye into the brain."

We reveal ourselves in our choices. "What a violent turn of mind you have," I tell him. I nod at the object in his hand. "It's exactly what it appears to be: a ring."

He frowns at the piece before returning it to the shelf. "Why the long spike? It seems rather strange for something you'd wear for adornment . . ."

"It serves a second purpose specific to the Damji. The might of their magic came from community. They worked only as a group, and the rod on that ring acted like a lightning rod, attenuating their power."

His eyebrows rise in surprise.

"It was really something to witness—or so I've heard. They were a powerful group for their time. And now lost forever. It only goes to show that time swallows us all: the great, the small, the strong, the weak."

He appears to regard the ring with greater appreciation now. "A group with a unique perspective on magic and how to wield it . . . A pity that there are no more Damji."

"Yes," I answer, doing my best to give away nothing. "They are all gone."

Except one.

I remember the first time I saw Badaal. I had just passed my Day of Attainment. As a Damji, I was now considered an adult. But by nearly any measure, I was not an adult. I was only starting to grow the long, sturdy legs of my people and beginning to gain my ability to see in the dark, which I needed to join the night hunts (hunting being best after the sun went down to lessen the possibility of heat stroke in our sun-blessed land).

I was home with members of my clan. Every Damji was considered to be part of one family. These women were my sisters, aunts, cousins, the men my brothers and uncles. My mother, the matriarch of our clan, was in consultation with the elders, her custom at this hour of the day. Several of the older children were preparing the evening meal, while the younger ones had been put to work in the form of a game: cutting dried leather into strips to braid into rope and netting. Everyone was working—except me.

I was being petulant, hiding up on the veranda where I could spy down on everyone else. I was afraid my life would soon be over, rather than just beginning. I would no longer be allowed to do as I pleased. A primary role would be selected for me soon, and then my life's direction would be set. I knew what the role would be: I was expected to be a leader of my people, like my mother. I wasn't sure if that was what I wanted—truthfully, if it was something I had in me. I had yet to be tested. Too, they would find a partner for me now among the others my age. Within a few years' time, I would marry. Everything would change soon, whether I wanted it to or not.

The only thing that would not change was our family's spiritual practice. Everyone in my clan was expected to be part of it. That was one thing I'd still be able to participate in: the magic of the Damji was shared equally by each member. It was specific and individual, yes, but here was the interesting thing about it, the *unique* thing: it was meant to be a shared experience. The more of us who practiced at the same time, the stronger the magic. That meant everyone in the family was encouraged to learn the magical art.

You can see why this would make other clans suspicious of us. Some were downright fearful. I'd overheard my father and uncles at night, gathered around the bonfire, talking about rival clans' jealousies. They envied our peacefulness. Our unity. Our magic, which could transmute one material into another. Other clans were frequently torn apart by jealousy and greed, the aspiration of the individual, the eternal hunger of the ego. Not so the Damji. As long as we stayed together, I figured, we were safe. We were strong.

I was on the veranda, hiding under a voluminous awning, when I heard a commotion. It came from the courtyard in the direction of the stables where the livestock were kept. It sounded like a fight had broken out among the group—which seemed unlikely. They were herding the livestock to make sure they were under cover for the hottest part of the day. There was little shade out on the savannah, and the intense sun could dehydrate a camel or ox in a few hours. No one wanted to be out in the midday heat even a minute longer than was necessary. Someone might get cranky, true, but they would work together in order to get the task done swiftly.

That was when I saw the flash of an explosion and heard the thunderclap.

It happened quickly after that. From the vantage point of the veranda, I saw men in unfamiliar garb, coats of many colors, emerge from around the barns, spell staffs raised high. They all wore red scarves to obscure their faces. A thick black plume of smoke was rising over the buildings, smelling of havoc and destruction. Then more explosions, more flashes of light, the smell of brimstone and hellfire and other impossible, profane ingredients. The young ones running, shouting. The clap of explosions at their backs, the cry of people dying.

Not just anyone: my brothers, sisters, aunts, uncles, and cousins. My father.

The people in the kitchen heard the explosions too and flew into a panic. But my mother, my calm, intelligent mother, a natural-born leader, began to organize them quickly. Outside, our kin did not have weapons with them, she knew. There was no reason to carry weapons with them to tend the livestock at midday. There were no predators in our valley.

We didn't think of the predators coming from outside. We didn't know how jealousy and fear could drive a person—or another clan—to do the unthinkable.

Why didn't my mother summon the clan to magic? A reasonable question. She was not wearing her ring. None of us were. It seemed unnecessary in the safety of our home, just as you wouldn't carry a crossbow to the dining table or bring vials of poison with you to bed.

My mother was rushing for her ring now, and urging the others to fetch theirs too.

They didn't get far before the front door flew open.

The men in those multicolored coats burst in, their staffs

raised and pointed at the members of my family. I expected they would order them to kneel on the floor or stand against the wall. I thought they'd come for young women. Bride-stealing was not uncommon, though usually it was done by one man, maybe with a friend or two for courage. I'd never heard of them coming for brides en masse like this.

But then they raised their staffs.

At first, I recoiled at the bloody, violent sight before my eyes, scrambling farther beneath the awning. Then, I wanted to try to rush to save them. I knew, though, there was nothing I could do. I should've remained hidden on the veranda, hoping to be mistaken for a pile of wash. But I knew I could not remain hidden. Better to die with the rest of my family than spend the rest of my days knowing that I was all alone in the universe because of my cowardice.

I threw off the awning and came out charging. I ran down the stairs and, with a mighty roar, threw myself at one of the attackers. It was a young man, no older than me. He seemed surprised. Their plan had gone so well. My family would never have expected to be attacked in their communal home like this. That's why we hadn't raised an aura of protection. We had been too trusting.

He almost fell backward at the sight of me. It was then I saw he had a staff. He was a mage too, then, but perhaps a neophyte, to go by his youth. He raised his staff and concentrated with all his might as he pointed it at me, reciting words I couldn't make out.

Centuries later, I still remember the pain that flooded through me. It was like I'd been set on fire, so intense that everything else—the screaming, the wailing, the smell of blood—disappeared. It was just me and a fire raging up the right side of my body.

I opened my eyes to find I was lying on the floor. I felt like I was floating. All around me a massacre was going on, but I could hear nothing, feel nothing. I couldn't move. I now know that I was in shock. The boy who had hurt me was leaning over me, wondering if I was dying.

My part of the pitched battle was over. I couldn't help anyone. I couldn't even help myself.

And then, over the boy's right shoulder, I saw Badaal. He made himself visible to me and only me. I would've been frightened, mistaking him for a demon or ghost, except for the look of extreme pity in his eyes. I can still picture him as I saw him that day. His bald head, so white that it looked bluish. His long black tunic sweeping down to his ankles. Those black pinprick eyes. And that look of great, great sadness.

Pretend you are dead. I heard his words in my head though his lips didn't move. *If you pretend you are dead, he will not hurt you again. He will believe you are dead too. I will make sure of it.*

I did as he instructed.

The last thing I saw was my mother die. She had crawled over my youngest sister to shield her. The man confronting them was not moved to pity and ran a blade into my mother's chest before slitting my sister's throat. I focused on his eyes, his cruel eyes. Killers, I have discovered over the millennia, all have the same eyes.

I pretended to be dead for hours. I lay perfectly still as my family's attackers celebrated throughout our bloody house. They nudged bodies with their boots to make sure all were dead. They dipped fingers into my sisters' wounds and smeared red across the foreheads of their youngest to signify their first kill.

After they left, Badaal materialized in the flesh. He carried me to another part of the house. He applied salve to my wounds, using a scrap of my attacker's red scarf to bandage them up.

"Who are you?" I asked, when the ability to speak returned.

He spoke kindly and moved with exquisite gentleness. "I was sent to record the event that took place today."

"The massacre." Even at that age, I knew it for what it was.

"Yes, the massacre."

"They weren't bandits. They didn't come to rob us. They were mages." I felt that I had to tell someone. That this fact must be made clear.

"You must forget that part—"

"Forget?" The words choked. "How can I forget?"

He placed his hands on mine, and their touch loosened something inside. Again, I was floating, gently being detached from the horror surrounding me. "All will be clear . . . in time.

In the meanwhile, I'm going to take you away from here. To someplace safe. Will you let me do this?"

Reluctantly, I nodded.

He bowed his head. "You may despise me for not acting, for doing nothing while . . ." Our thoughts went to the bodies cooling not thirty yards away. "But it was not in my power. It was not my role. You see, I am a Hedaji. We are forbidden from acting—even in the annihilation of an entire clan. Sadly, such events are not uncommon in the history of the universe. I was only there to do my job—to record. To witness."

I touched his hand as he tied the bandage. "And yet, you did act."

He smiled. "I saw you throw yourself at the attackers, and I knew in that moment that what I was witnessing was not Fate. It was not Destiny. At this instant, time presented itself in two ways, like a fork in the path of time. If you lived, you would do something great." I am not flattering myself: this was something Badaal had seen. I would not know until much later that Badaal was a seer of great power.

He couldn't ignore this feeling. He had to save me.

"It is beyond my power to save you, unless you become Hedaji. That is the only action we are allowed to take: we can intervene if we find a candidate suitable to join us." His eyes smiled as he looked on me. "And you would be an outstanding candidate.

"Besides, it would be safest. You will be hidden, for the most part. No one will be able to see you unless you let them. Given what has happened to your family, I think you will agree that no one *should* see you right now. No one should know that anyone from your clan survived this day. Not until you know who is behind it and why they wanted your family killed."

"But if you can see everything, you must know who these people are and why they did this," I told him.

Badaal turned away from me. "Part of the curse of being Hedaji is . . . knowledge. Life in the order is not easy, Tejal. Details will be shared with you . . . You will be witness to the heartbreaking and the horrendous. The basic fabric of the universe is not kindness. The universe is blind to suffering. And you must stand witness to it all. You must obey your limitations. You must never act, and there is a reason for this."

"How do you handle it?" I asked. I would come to know Badaal well, for we were to spend much time together. I know him to be a decent, kind individual. But that day, I wondered if he was some kind of monster.

"You learn to accept what you cannot control. If you have faith in the importance of the mission, you understand that it must be done. We cannot all be great heroes. However, without the Hedaji, without scribes, there would be no perfectly complete record of many of humanity's heroic deeds. It would be as though those heroic feats never happened."

But that day—breaking his oath to rescue me—Badaal had dared to be a hero.

I listened to Badaal. I accepted his offer and dedicated myself to the Hedaji. At first, I did it because it was a solution to my conundrum. Too, I felt I owed it to Badaal for saving me. It was only in the fullness of time that I came to truly embrace my duty. My obligation. To come to see it as my calling.

Which is not to say that the restrictions never chafed. Under the hood and ink, I was still human. I had a heart and was still capable of emotion.

Giaran is making me nervous. It is the first time I can remember feeling this way in a long, long time. After all, I am protected.

I push back from the table. "You came here because you are looking for something. Why don't you tell me, and we can stop playing games?"

He'll be angered by my words, I think. Or maybe I misunderstood him. He might not have known what he wanted—some people hide their deepest desires from even themselves. Sometimes they are too shy or embarrassed to ask for it.

But then I follow his gaze and know exactly what he is looking for.

He is staring at the space between my breasts.

This has nothing to do with lust, however. Nestled between my breasts is an artifact, worn like a pendant on a leather thong. It is a heavy, shaped piece of iron.

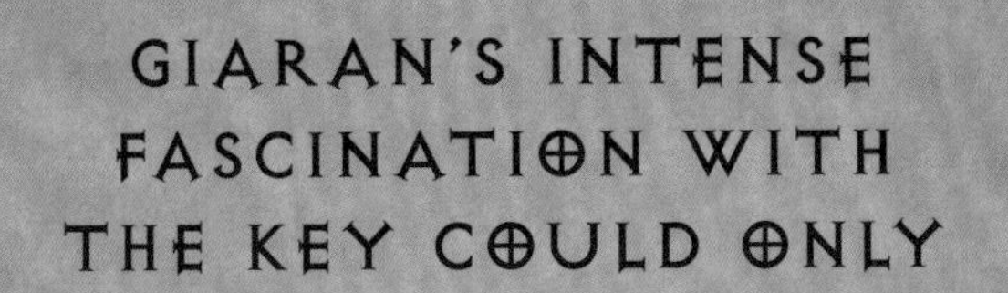

GIARAN'S INTENSE
FASCINATION WITH
THE KEY COULD ONLY

MEAN ONE THING:
HE WAS SENT
TO KILL ME.

A key. A common key, the kind that looks like it could open a simply made door at a tavern somewhere. A key so ordinary that there is no reason for the stranger to gape at it.

Unless Giaran knows what it is, knows which door it opens.

I wager he does.

He hasn't come for the ring. The ring was merely a test. It proved I knew about the Damji—intimately. No, he has come for the key.

The key unlocks the vault that holds my most important secret. It was hidden by a witch from Hawezar who performed a spell for me. I had argued with the witch that I would keep my secret hidden, but she insisted it would be safer if it was hidden by a second party. If I didn't know where it was hidden, I would never be able to reveal it under the pain of torture, would I?

The compromise was that the witch gave me the key. Now anyone who wanted me dead would need to go through two steps: find out where this secret talisman had been hidden, and then wrest the key away from me—and not necessarily in that order.

It had seemed a good plan. It has managed to keep me immortal all these centuries.

What I hadn't counted on then, being much younger and less experienced when the spell was cast, is that witches can be—and are—bribed. On a frighteningly regular basis.

Giaran's intense fascination with the key could only mean one thing: he was sent to kill me.

As I look into his blue eyes, it falls into place. I have seen his type before. He is an assassin, a mercenary killer. Those killer's eyes have given him away. Someone saw the Damji ring in my collection and figured out that not all Damji had been wiped out that terrible day. One had escaped through extraordinary, unforeseen measures.

Why now? Why would anyone send a paid assassin to scour the universe to find me? Assassins of this caliber do not come cheaply. I can imagine a number of reasons someone would want me dead. Perhaps I stood by and let someone's loved one die, someone's mother or father or infant daughter.

Though it is unlikely they would be able to pin me to their deaths. No one can see a Hedaji while they are scribing.

No, this grudge comes from the time before I joined the Hedaji.

Which leads back to the slaughter of the Damji.

I never learned who was behind the attack on my family. Badaal insisted that I let it go, that I refuse to retain such a damaging memory in my consciousness. If I didn't let it go, he warned, I would never heal. He knew he was asking a lot, but it would prove I had the self-control and discipline to be a Hedaji, maybe to be the best Hedaji of them all.

It was hard, but I closed the door on that one curiosity. After all, satisfying that curiosity would not bring them back. I would not be any less alone.

Now, centuries later, I see that whatever feud brought about my family's massacre was not over. It would not be over until the last Damji was dead.

Or perhaps the point was to eliminate the ability to tell what had happened. *To bear witness. To give testimony.*

Could Giaran have been sent to kill me so that the slaughter of my family will remain in the past? Someone—possibly a clan or family—wanting their guilt to remain hidden? My father had argued with several powerful clans. Any of them could be responsible. Jealous, or greedy to learn about our techniques, our special abilities that could do things like turn metal into gold.

All these thoughts come to me in a rush, maybe because I've carried them in the back of my mind. Badaal understood from the very beginning: I must remain hidden. Someone might come looking for me. It's safer this way, hidden as a Hedaji.

He was right—but it seems my attraction for artifacts has been my undoing.

But there is also a weakness of the Hedaji: we are solitary creatures. We live alone.

And living alone, there is no one there to hear your screams as you die.

Giaran sees my eye on him. He knows that I am on to him.

My options flash by in a moment. I could fight for my life. We are in my home. I have the advantage. He doesn't know if someone might come by, if another customer might appear in a swirl of mist. He doesn't know what deadly artifacts hang on my walls, weapons I could call to my hand in an instant.

Whatever he may know of me is undoubtedly limited.

I don't deceive myself, though: he is a paid assassin.

He's seen my missing finger and drawn the correct conclusion: I am protected by a spell of immortality.

He is in possession of all *his* digits, so unless he's protected by some other spell or amulet, he is vulnerable—provided I can get close enough to kill him. But that seems unlikely.

None of my options look good. The most likely outcome is that he'll take me prisoner until he's able to break the spell. At which point, he'll kill me. There's the chance that I'll simply dissolve into dust once the spell is broken, returning to my organic state and surrendering to the strictures of time.

I understand now this feeling I've had since he materialized in my parlor: Giaran came with bad intent. It may be the beginning of my end. My heart speeds up. Sweat breaks out on my upper lip, even though I know that I'm not going to die just yet.

And then: cool detachment crashes over me like an ocean wave. It's the Hedaji's gift, the ability to simply observe without judging or feeling the need to come up with a solution. I see this moment for what it is, part of a chain that started when my family was killed and Badaal decided to intervene. It was inevitable that, one day, the circle would come around and I would be back at this spot. The events of that day would one day either lead to my death or the ability to avenge my family.

The Hedaji do not recognize vengeance, however.

I was Damji once, a very long time ago.

But I am Hedaji *now.*

It as though time is frozen. Giaran continues to study me, trying to discern what I am thinking. I am calculating what my next move *must* be, because there will be no second chances.

I could kill him. The urge to preserve oneself is strong. It feels foreign because I have not had such a thought in a long time. Being protected, it simply wasn't needed. This is different. If I kill this man, my future is secured. At least until the next assassin finds me.

I can picture how to take this man's life. I can hurl myself at him, shove him against the wall. Affixed in a display on the wall is a dagger that once belonged to a rogue necromancer. The bone blade may no longer be razor sharp, but with enough force applied behind it, it could punch through a man's ribs. The stranger has a sword and who knows what else hidden on his person, but I would have the element of surprise, and the protection spell would slow his hand, make him fumble with the sword's sheath, delay him enough to give me time to strike.

Blood thrums in my ears. *I could kill him, but is it permitted?* His death could change the course of time.

Before I can address this question, however, the decision is taken out of my hands.

He moves more quickly than I imagined possible. Before I can bat an eye, he has leapt on me, vaulting over the table with the litheness of a jungle cat. We tumble to the floor, his weight pinning me down. For such a slender man, he's surprisingly heavy. He's all muscle and bone.

I try to engage his hands to keep him from reaching for his sword or a hidden dagger. He might not be able to kill me outright, but he can wound me, make it impossible for me to defend myself. I don't want to end up bound and gagged.

We wrestle, but it will only be a matter of time before I tire, and I know I will tire before he does. I can see now how strong he is. I underestimated him earlier, put too much faith in the protection spell.

He grips my bodice and shakes me. Every yank makes the tight straps dig into my ribs and spine. I weaken fast as the last of my oxygen is squeezed out of my lungs. I grapple frantically with his hands, trying to break his hold, but to no avail.

He is staring at the key. His fixation is total, practically burning my flesh.

It's only then I remember and realize: *let him take the key.*

I lessen my grip on his wrists and he breaks free, thinking I've made a mistake or I'm exhausted. He grabs the key, snapping the thong with one forceful jerk.

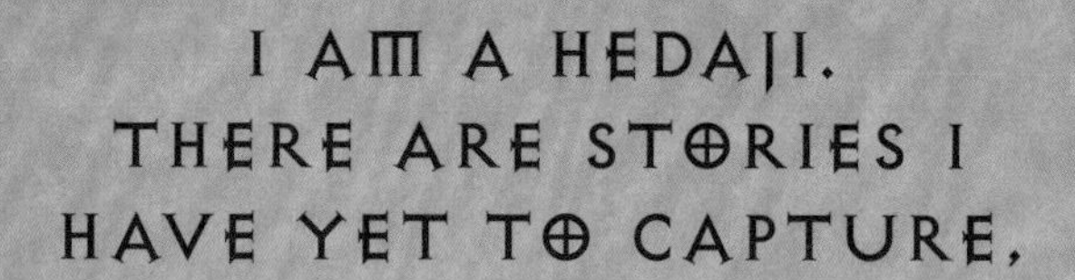

I AM A HEDAJI.
THERE ARE STORIES I
HAVE YET TO CAPTURE,

DOWN TO
THE EXACTING
DETAILS.

With the last bit of my strength, I cast a spell that impels me away from him. It gives me only a few feet of separation but at the same time envelops me in a protective aura. It won't last long, but I pray it will be deterrent enough.

He rises woozily from the floor. He stares at the key in his hand, not believing his good luck. Then he looks up at me. I'm visible behind the fog. I cringe on the floor, as though I'm helpless.

I need to convince him that I'm not a threat.

He curls a lip and shoves the key inside his coat. I'm sure he would prefer to bring me with him. It would be the most prudent thing to do. But right now, I'm behind a shield he cannot pierce, and he knows that he doesn't need to bring me with him. My life may end when the spell is lifted, or he can simply track me down again and finish the job. So, at this moment, he'll take the less sure way because it's easier and he wants to get this damn job over with and move on to the next.

He disappears in a cloud of mist.

I breathe a sigh of relief.

What he doesn't know—what I only just remembered—is that the key is cursed. I wrapped it in a spell that will destroy whoever tries to use it. It's risky . . . By doing so, I condemned myself to immortality. It wasn't because I wanted to live forever—I feared it, actually, having spoken once to a wizard who had done the same thing and lived to regret it, wizened and more resembling a turtle than a man.

He, too, had been alone in the universe, everyone he knew dead.

Unlike the old wizard, however, I had something to live for. I am a Hedaji. There are stories I have yet to capture, down to the exacting details.

I rise from the floor, testing my aching joints, readjusting the straps of my bodice. The urge to follow Giaran is strong—but pointless. There is no need. When he tries to use the key, he will be destroyed, and I can retrieve the key. I am safe . . . but it's hard to believe it, especially after grappling with the man for my life. It takes a long time for my breathing to return to normal, for my mind to stop racing and to turn the facts over slowly and precisely.

Someone from my deep past, my Damji past, wants me dead. They will not succeed this time. Will they try again? I walk to the shelves and pick up that scrap of fabric Badaal cleverly left with me hundreds of years ago. The means to find them has always been with me. It's been my choice not to pursue them. If that situation should ever change, well . . . I am in a good position to watch. Hedaji are spies, the best spies in all the worlds. Now that I know the peril I am in, I will watch.

The air begins to shimmer. Another visitor is coming.

I hurry to set right the furniture that was knocked aside, to conjure an air of calm onto the room. It's hard to force an air of calm upon myself, however.

The fog swirls, then parts, and another visitor stands in the center of my parlor. I arrange a smile on my face.

"Welcome, stranger! Shall we see what destiny has in store for you today?"

Sanctum of Bone

A SHORT STORY BY

CARLY ANNE WEST

SANCTUM OF BONE

Upon the backs of stormy winds, the tortured screams escaped the moors of Scosglen like shrikes bursting from the knotted tree line. They were nothing like the howls of lycan myth that had come to plague the moors. No, these were cries of an unnatural sort. This was the sound of unjust death, of innocent blood spilled upon tainted soil. The place was the sanctum, and its headmaster preyed upon Sanctuary's most vulnerable—the poor and wandering children.

I, Tejal, have heard the echoes of their cries in my dreams. I will tell you the story of their origin, but be warned, for this tale is treacherous as it expounds upon the legend of how a most fearsome set of armor came to be.

While the one who imbued it with righteous service to the Balance ultimately came to bear its heavy burden, this armor's rotted seed runs bone-deep. Quietly now, light a candle and gather closely as I uproot the armor's decrepit past. Thin is the veil that separates the craving for knowledge and the hunger for power . . .

Iolaynah stared out at the sanctum below, standing sentinel over the Scosglen moors, overtaken though it was by the towering trees encircling the dark stone walls. Tree roots erupted from the ground, cracking the walkway beneath the arched iron entrance.

Iolaynah stepped carefully. Rumors had placed the sanctum on the periphery of the moors, but as she stood staring up at the imposing castle, it looked more like an outcropping of Scosglen than a place for study built along its edge.

"I'm here, Lorameere," Iolaynah whispered. She had traveled far to find her sister, and she wouldn't let anything stand against her.

Lorameere was barely a toddler when she was taken into Iolaynah's traveling caravan as a refugee, raised alongside Iolaynah by her father. A band of misfit entertainers, their troupe performed for the local taverners, sea-haggard sailors, and awestruck children, who squinted to discern sleight of hand from true magic.

Iolaynah and Lorameere never spent more than a few hours apart in their years as a little family. Thieves had taken their father from them years ago in a raid that decimated their troupe. They buried his remains among the oil pits of Kehjistan, the only funeral two little girls with no father could make, and each took an inheritance—her father's prized dagger with the jewel embedded deep in its hilt for Iolaynah, and a green silk bow for Lorameere, the one that had belonged to Iolaynah's mother. They were even closer then, these twice-orphaned sisters, traveling with the troupe, performing their act. Until Lorameere went away to study at the sanctum one year ago. Until her letter announcing her arrival six months later.

Until the silence that followed.

Iolaynah's first rap of the heavy brass knocker went unanswered. She strained to hear rustlings of life inside the imposing castle. She knocked again but was met with only an echo of the clang.

Stepping back, she tried peering into the small square windows, but they were too few and deeply inset, giving the illusion of hooded, unblinking eyes. Abandoning the knocker, Iolaynah balled her hand into a fist and pounded hard. This time, the door gave way.

Stepping into a dim foyer, Iolaynah expected to look upon the gilded furnishings and elegant carvings of some esteemed house of learning. Instead, she could scarcely breathe through the layers of decay and mold. The same roots breaking through the walkway outside had pried open the mortar between the stones in the walls. Vines twisted along the rails adorning a grand staircase, writhing snakes frozen in time. A damp chill had settled so deeply in the air, Iolaynah scarcely recognized she had left the outdoors; inside, it was as cold and dark as night.

With an echoing thud, the wooden door shut, and when Iolaynah turned, she gasped to find a stooped, hooded figure standing behind her. She reached for the hilt of her dagger tucked snugly in its leather sheath at her waist. At closer glance, she relaxed her grip; the boy wasn't a threat. If anything, he was afraid of *her.*

The ragged cloak hung about his thin form like a rag on a cross in a cornfield. His spine was twisted, and though his face was wreathed in shadow, Iolaynah could still make out the hollowness of his cheeks, his sunken eyes, his teeth protruding against dry, cracked lips. A map of fine scars traced their way across his pale, exposed skin.

"I-I thank you for your hospitality," Iolaynah stuttered. Where in the Hells had she let Lorameere be taken to?

The boy avoided her eyes, instead glancing nervously around the foyer. Iolaynah followed his gaze, but all she could see beyond the dust and moldering rafters were shadowy corridors to nowhere.

When the boy said nothing, Iolaynah forced herself to recall the story she had planned to tell.

"Tapestries!" she said abruptly. "I come bearing tapestries. Or rather, my mistress has sent me from Kehjistan to the finest castles and cities in search of buyers for our rare and luxurious textiles. Might I speak with—"

"Leave!" the boy hissed, lunging at Iolaynah with frightening

speed, grasping her arm and pushing her toward the heavy door. "You must leave here at once!"

"What are you—I don't understand," Iolaynah protested, struggling against the boy's frantic efforts.

"You should never have come!" the boy whispered. He was leaning his entire pathetic weight on her now, but he was no match for Iolaynah. Whatever ill fortune had befallen this boy, she wasn't about to let it happen to Lorameere too.

"I'm looking for my friend," she whispered back to the boy, dropping the ruse. "She's tall, much taller than me," she said, "with long black hair she wears in a braid with a green ribbon. Always with a green ribbon. Her name is Lorameere. Please, you must tell me if you know her—"

"*Go!*" The boy's desperation was tangible.

Suddenly, he dropped Iolaynah's arm and stepped away from her, lowering his gaze.

"Elden, you should have told me we had a visitor," said a voice deep enough to fill the cavernous space of the foyer.

The boy shook violently at the sound of the cloaked figure looming at the top of the grand staircase.

A mercurial aura followed the man as he descended the stairs. His finely appointed robes covered every inch of his skin—even his hands—but his hood remained at the back of his neck, exposing a warm face split by a wide smile.

"My apologies for the intrusion." Iolaynah bowed. "I am but

a humble merchant who would be grateful for a night's stay and some nourishment, if the headmaster would be amenable to such a request."

The man laughed. "I assure you, the headmaster would insist you take refuge here for the night."

As he reached the bottom of the stairs, the man gripped the knob of the banister in a way that reminded her of the grip she had so often held on the knife in her sheath. The banister's ornament was orb-shaped and ivory-colored, identical to the one on the opposite banister, precisely the size of the man's fist. Smooth as a finely formed skull.

"Are you certain?" Iolaynah asked warily. "Perhaps I should inquire directly," she pressed.

If anyone knows what's become of Lorameere, Iolaynah thought, *it will be the headmaster.* He was, after all, the one who had penned her invitation to study here.

The man in the silk cloak took Iolaynah's hand.

"Headmaster Droman Grigso. A pleasure to make your acquaintance."

Iolaynah forced a smile to her lips, stunned into silence. Lorameere had spoken much of Grigso, the sanctum's headmaster and founder, before she left. Surely his age would far exceed that of the person who approached her now, a man of no more than thirty by Iolaynah's estimate. Releasing her hand, Grigso moved on to the trembling boy beside her.

"Elden, I believe you're needed in the greenhouse," the headmaster said calmly.

"Sir, i-if it wouldn't be too much trouble, could I show our guest to her q-q-quarters first?"

"Now, Elden . . ." The headmaster placed his hand on the boy's shoulder and squeezed.

Iolaynah realized with a growing dread that the control Grigso had over the boy was absolute. Elden offered no further protest. He simply turned on his heel, loosened his clenched fists, and walked down one of the long, dark corridors leading away from the foyer, disappearing into the shadows.

Grigso smiled. "My apologies for the interruption."

"It's no trouble!" Iolaynah tittered, remembering her story. "I come to you on behalf of my mistress, the finest tapestry weaver in Kurast. She heard tell that your fine sanctum was perhaps in need of . . ." Here, Iolaynah trod carefully, worried she would offend the headmaster.

Grigso grinned. "About restoring this house of learning to its former glory?"

Iolaynah wanted to be comforted by the headmaster's smile. If only the light of it had reached his eyes. Yet just as the whole of the castle lurked in shadow, so too did Grigso's countenance. She suspected there was more hiding behind Grigso's smile than there was in the endless hallways winding throughout the sanctum.

Iolaynah demurred. “Perhaps the scholars here would benefit from a reinvigorated interior.”

Grigso’s smile remained, but his eyes searched her, and she worried she had left some part of herself exposed. Had he seen through her ruse?

“Surely you know our numbers have . . . waned over the years,” Grigso said slowly. “Such a shame,” he said, shaking his head. “So few minds touched with that rare combination of natural magical ability and the curiosity to test its limits.”

Iolaynah cleared her throat. “Yes, such a shame, Headmaster.”

Silence thickened between them.

To her relief, Grigso turned away, heading back up the grand staircase as he set forth a proposal. “I’m inclined to entertain your offer,” he said as Iolaynah followed behind him.

“You would be interested in fabrics, then? Some damask silks? Perhaps I can look around to get a feel for the decor. You needn’t accompany me. Surely you have more important—”

“We can discuss specifics later,” Grigso answered, leading her to the highest level of the sanctum. “You were right to seek lodging here. The night grows dark, and it would be imprudent to journey at this late hour. We have more than enough space in our students’ quarters.”

“That’s very kind of you,” Iolaynah might have said had she not been so distracted by the scene before her: The corridor he gestured toward was wholly abandoned.

It was evident this darkened, cobwebbed hall hadn't been used in months . . . maybe years. The musty stench alone betrayed its neglect and seclusion from the rest of the sanctum.

From where Iolaynah stood, it looked as though the only door that wasn't covered in cobwebs was the one to their immediate left—the one Droman Grigso was unlocking with the key he pulled from the folds of his robe.

Before he could unlock the door, a distant but unmistakable scream echoed through the castle, cracking the silence that blanketed the corridor.

Iolaynah sucked in a sharp breath, instinctively reaching for her dagger.

To her surprise, Grigso merely chuckled.

"Dreadful, aren't they? Awful wailings. I thought I'd go mad when I first heard them."

"Where are they coming from? Is someone—"

Grigso coolly dismissed her. "Some sort of creature from the moors, I assume. Another unfortunate by-product of our proximity to such an unsavory place," he lamented. "Beasts baying at the bloody moon or some nonsense."

The dormitory door swung open to a sloped stone floor and a small, spare room furnished with a straw-stuffed mattress, a table with a basin, an empty wardrobe in the corner, and a window with a view obscured entirely by an imposing tree trunk directly outside.

Iolaynah stepped cautiously into the room. She could feel Grigso's eyes on her back. She approached her next question with care. "Are many of the chambers occupied?"

A pause long enough to grow uncomfortable followed, and Iolaynah eventually turned to face the headmaster. That same empty smile. The same hollow eyes. Iolaynah suppressed a shiver.

"A few here and there. You've met Elden, of course," Grigso replied, still grinning. "We like to keep our finest minds close at hand to . . . keep the conversation well nourished. A starved mind dies a slow death."

Iolaynah nodded, again noting the perfectly smooth skin framing his features.

The second Grigso closed the door behind him, Iolaynah collapsed onto the bare mattress, filling her lungs with the musty air of the tiny room. She couldn't remember feeling such relief as she did the second she was out of the headmaster's company. There remained not a single doubt in her mind that Lorameere was in terrible danger, wherever she was in the enormous castle. From the little she'd seen of the sanctum, the long, winding corridors could number in the dozens. It could take her weeks to search the entirety of the place. If she had any hope of finding Lorameere, she needed a sign, something to point her in the right direction.

She stepped toward the window and put her fingertips to the glass, then slid them to the gnarled branch that had wound its

THERE REMAINED
NOT A SINGLE DOUBT
IN HER MIND THAT
LORAMEERE

WAS IN TERRIBLE
DANGER, WHEREVER
SHE WAS IN THE
ENORMOUS CASTLE.

way inside, surprised by the warmth of it despite the chill that permeated the air outside. Pressing her face to the pane, she looked down to discover it wasn't a branch at all, but a stray root that had erupted from the ground and climbed the wall of the castle. Holding her fingers to the root, she swore she could feel a thumping deep within its core.

No, not a thumping . . . a *pulsing*. Like a heartbeat.

Iolaynah snatched her hand away.

"Lorameere," Iolaynah whispered. "Show me where you are. Show me how to find you."

Suddenly, a low groan beside Iolaynah stopped her racing heart, and from the corner of her eye, she saw the door of the wardrobe slowly hang farther open.

Iolaynah crept toward the open wardrobe, but when she peered inside, she found only an empty wooden closet.

Perhaps she's in one of the other chambers, Iolaynah thought.

Carefully, she peered down the hallway, then quietly tried the neighboring door. The knob refused to turn, so she slid her dagger from its sheath and freed the spindle from its hold.

The scene inside was a cobwebbed tomb from some unknown time. The scattered papers on the table lay under a thick pile of dust, the basin beside the bed was cracked and dry, and the mattress smelled of mildew. Secured to the stone wall by an invading root was a framed portrait of two girls, arms encircling each other, cheeks pressed together as they smiled.

"Which one of them was you?" she asked the room.

Crossing the hall, she pried the lock open to the next dormitory and found a similar scene, this room clearly abandoned as hastily as the previous one: tomes splayed across the bed, a pile of unfolded clothes in a corner, a half-finished meal, now only petrified remnants.

Iolaynah had seen enough. She backed out of the room, easing the door shut behind her. Just as she turned to slink back to her room, Iolaynah gasped. Disappearing into the doorway to her room was a long green ribbon at the tail of a black waist-length braid.

Iolaynah crossed the corridor in three leaps, but when she entered her room, she found it as empty as she'd left it.

"Lorameere?"

She searched the dormitory frantically, opening and closing the wardrobe, ducking under the table, peering out the sealed window—all of them impossible places for Lorameere to hide, but *she had seen her.* She was certain of it.

Just as Iolaynah prepared to look over the landing of the grand staircase, she was met at the top of the steps by a shrouded, pale face.

"Oh! Elden, you startled— Did Lorameere pass you just now on the stairs? She must have!"

"The headmaster would enjoy your company in the dining hall for supper," he said flatly.

Iolaynah tried to understand. Had he not heard her? "Elden, I need your help. I think she's in terrible danger!" She stared hard at the boy, whose eyes were lost in the shadows of his cloak.

His voice betrayed not an ounce of life. "The headmaster will expect you at half eight."

With that, Elden turned, and with his limping gait, made his pained way down the grand staircase before the dark swallowed him back up once again.

The table was set for two: one end for Grigso, the other for Iolaynah. Elden finished placing covered dishes before them, then departed.

"Just us, then?" Iolaynah asked as she took her seat in an upholstered, high-backed chair. "I'd hoped perhaps some scholars or students might be joining us."

She struggled to keep her tone casual, but she was still vibrating from her near encounter with Lorameere. She was certain she'd seen her.

Grigso's hollow smile spread across his face as he locked eyes with Iolaynah.

"I took the liberty of choosing tonight's menu," he said, pointedly ignoring her comment. "I trust it will be to your satisfaction."

Testing her luck, Iolaynah tried a different angle.

"These invasive roots have made quite a mess of your tapestries," she said, gesturing toward the walls with their cracked mortar and their serpentine intruders. "Perhaps your young protégé, Elden, might show me the areas of the sanctum in need of the most attention—"

To her astonishment, Grigso burst into bellowing laughter.

"Dear girl, are you still playing at that charade?" Grigso taunted, dabbing at the corners of his eyes with his cloak.

Iolaynah swallowed hard, waiting to see what Grigso would do next. She only dared exhale when Grigso smoothly lifted his wineglass to take a drink, set the glass back down, then uncovered his dish. The steam from the food before him made the air shimmer.

"Please." He gestured to her to do the same as the steam dissipated.

She slowly lifted her own covering and waited for the food to cool, fork in hand. She recognized the smooth handle of the cutlery immediately—it felt just like holding her father's dagger. Staring down at her place setting, she saw the handles of the knife and spoon laid before her, like the fork, were carved of the same smooth ivory as the ornaments decorating the heads of the banisters. The stems of the wineglasses too.

When the steam from her plate cleared, Iolaynah saw what lay before her. She forced herself to stare at it, to smile through her teeth, masking her revulsion.

"Thank you," she said, her voice quieter than she'd meant for it to be.

"Jellied cuttlefish ink sac atop a bed of boiled local greens," he rattled off casually. "Those roots of which you just spoke, in fact," he mused. "They are indeed invasive, though I must say, their persistence is impressive. I find myself continuing to count their uses."

Something in Grigso's tone made Iolaynah doubt he was referring to the roots' nutritional value. Besides, they were the least offensive offering on the plate. The jelly bore a horrifying likeness to the very oil pits by which Lorameere and Iolaynah had held their father's meager funeral. Rare meat sat in piles speared by their own sharp bones, tiny as toothpicks in some places, sharp enough to slice her throat if she swallowed them. Watery blood pooled to the plate's edge.

"Did you know that the northern saw-toothed venomous shrew eats nearly three times her body weight?" Grigso mused, forking a mouthful of the rare shrew meat into his mouth. A dribble of blood rolled down his chin.

Iolaynah's stomach churned as she thought she identified a tiny hindquarter tangled amid the roots on her dish.

"Remarkable little creatures. They've been known to keep their prey alive whilst feeding on them for up to three weeks," he continued, never breaking eye contact with Iolaynah.

Remember why you're here, she told herself. *Remember Lorameere.*

"Fascinating," Iolaynah said, playing along. "I recall you mentioning to Elden a greenhouse onsite as well. For the study of . . . local flora? Herbal remedies? Perhaps that's what occupies your students now?"

Fine if he knows I'm no merchant, she thought. *So long as he realizes I'm no fool, either. We both know this place is anything but a sanctum.*

Grigso's eyes widened, and he leaned forward, licking his lips.

"How very observant of you, my dear," he said, tilting his head slowly. "Aren't you the clever one?"

Iolaynah's stomach tightened, but she returned his smile with only a slow blink.

"Is it possible I've discovered your true reason for seeking an audience with me?" he posited. "You wouldn't be the first 'wayward traveler' to cross my path. My dear, if you wanted to study under my tutelage, you needn't have gone to such lengths."

Grigso chuckled as he ate, but Iolaynah feigned contrition. She recognized an opportunity when she saw one.

"I would offer my apologies, Headmaster, but might I be bold enough to assume I'm forgiven? Seeing as you've been so kind as to share your table with me?"

Grigso took a long draw from his wineglass. Iolaynah watched as his Adam's apple slid up and down his smooth, uncreased neck.

"I'll accept your apology in exchange for your name."

"Iolaynah," she admitted. She had nothing to lose in revealing that much.

IOLAYNAH'S STOMACH TWISTED INTO A KNOT.

"IT ISN'T TOO LATE. TELL ME WHERE TO FIND HER."

"And in answer to your question," he continued, "we do indeed pay close attention to the living and dying of things here. I wonder, have you ever thought it . . . arbitrary? How fleeting the existence for one life, how lasting for another? How quickly a promising life can be snatched away before its full potential is reached, by way of anomaly? A venomous mammal. The swing of a scythe. The curse of a deadly ailment. Tell me," he continued, his voice echoing in Iolaynah's ears, "have you never witnessed the long fingers of life close too soon around someone you love?"

Her father's dagger. The hole in the ground between the Kehjistani oil pits. Their pitiful funeral for such a great man.

"Such is the way of the Balance," she said, but they felt like someone else's words.

"Ah yes," Grigso said slowly. "The Balance. Yet have you never wondered why such important matters—the length of one's life—should be left to mere chance?"

For a moment, the sound of Droman Grigso's voice receded as Iolaynah's heartbeat thrummed hard in her ears.

No, she realized with horror. *Not* my *heartbeat.*

It was the collective heartbeat within the tangled roots twisting through the sanctum walls that she was hearing.

Iolaynah was so consumed by the thrumming heartbeat and violent visions of her past that she scarcely noticed Elden return to the dining hall. Only Grigso's sharp reprimand broke her disquieting hypnosis.

“You fool!” he hissed at Elden, who flinched under the headmaster’s scolding.

“I’m sorry, sir. I think they’re only a little burnt,” Elden said, trembling.

Grigso shoved him away. “I must check on our tartes.” He frowned. “It seems they’ve spent a bit too long over the fire.”

Iolaynah opened her mouth to decline the dessert and spare poor Elden, but Grigso was gone before she could say a word. To her shock, Elden sprinted toward Iolaynah the moment Grigso disappeared, pulling her out of the dining hall and into a dark alcove.

“It *was* Lorameere you saw,” he said breathlessly. “If she’d waited, I might have—but now he’s caught her and—”

“Elden, slow down.” Iolaynah took the boy by his bony shoulders.

Elden shook his head in quick snaps. “There isn’t time. She’ll be dead by morning. She should have waited for me to help her.”

Iolaynah’s stomach twisted into a knot. “It isn’t too late. Tell me where to find her.”

“The wardrobe in your room,” he said. “I can distract him while you—”

Elden’s eyes widened as they fixed on something. Iolaynah spun around, but when she couldn’t see anything behind her, she turned back to find the boy backed against a far wall, slinking away from her.

"What is it?" she asked Elden.

"You're the same as him," he said, his voice cracking.

"Who?"

Then she followed his gaze to her waistband and found her sheathed dagger. Still, she struggled to understand.

"Elden, it's for protection. You can't believe I would want to hurt you—"

"You're like him!" he cried, and before Iolaynah could say another word, Elden fled into the shadows, leaving her alone and confused.

She briefly considered running after him, but what if there wasn't time?

She'll be dead by morning.

That's what Elden had said.

Iolaynah raced up the grand staircase, swinging open the door to her room and this time stepping inside the wardrobe. Groping the roughly hewn wood, she slid her fingers back and forth, feeling for any irregularity in the fittings. At last, her thumb brushed against a strange curvature on the back wall, and her heart leapt as she felt a tiny latch. A section of the wall fell, creating a hole barely wide enough for Iolaynah to wriggle through on her stomach.

A dank, narrow passage greeted Iolaynah on the other side. The smell of mold clung to the air as she reached for the single torch, already lit and resting in a nearby sconce on the wall. She was disquieted by the torch, the thought that it was there, waiting for her.

It means Lorameere left it for you, she told herself. *It means she's still alive.*

Still, the passage only grew narrower the farther she traveled, squeezing her heart like how the tunnel squeezed her shoulders, until finally, she reached the end of the corridor and found a steeply winding staircase.

The stone staircase spiraled for what felt like a hundred floors. Between the mildew and the dizzying turns, Iolaynah nearly retched twice before her feet found the bottom.

Holding her torch high to light the bowels of the sanctum, Iolaynah did retch this time. Because what she found at the bottom of the staircase was a catacomb.

Hollow eye sockets and bared teeth haunted her in scattered rows, intersected by bones of all shapes and lengths, varying yellows and browns and states of decay. Tree roots had woven their way through the sockets of the skulls like serpents wrapping prey in a deadly embrace.

This place, this supposed sanctum of learning, was a house of death.

Still she continued, rounding the first corner as it bent to the right, and any worries that she was being led astray fell to pieces. On the path before her lay a small green ribbon, a few long black hairs tangled in the knot at the center of a loosened bow.

Iolaynah crouched to retrieve the satin ribbon. "I'm coming, Lorameere."

At last, the path of skulls and bones and roots halted at a small arched door, behind which emanated the sounds she could no longer deny were coming from the sanctum. Slowly, she opened the door to a fresh nightmare, and the true sources of the wailing screams unfolded.

A high-ceilinged dungeon towered above her, but these walls weren't the scattered bones and skulls of the ancient dead; these were the whole husks of hundreds of lives torn from their bodies. Mummified into grotesque rigor mortis and twisted with the agony of their final breaths, these human shells stood stacked between mortar and the snaking roots of the moors. From every corner, she could see the slow stages of death hard at work on what were once the students of the sanctum.

Against one wall, bound tightly to the human husks by pulsating roots, a man of no more than thirty years was splayed half-alive, his skin already putrefying. He was still alive to feel the piercing of the roots' needles, though, and the torturously long process of organic decay. On an adjacent wall, a young girl hung suspended by her ankles, dehydrated like an old bouquet of flowers, blackened and leathery, but to Iolaynah's horror, still blinking. On yet another wall, Iolaynah could see the legs and torso of a young boy, his upper body wrapped tightly in a ball of knotted roots; the only evidence he still breathed was the twitching of his small feet in midair.

In the center of the dungeon stood a pedestal, atop which sat a wooden trophy carved from the severed trunk of a tree. The statuette's jagged edges formed a cracked rib cage around a collection of yellowed skulls, each a face frozen in eternal agony. Roped with a totem of ivory and two copper bells, the macabre trophy was one that struck a deep memory in Iolaynah, one too ancient for her mind to retrieve.

"I had hoped to have a bit more time with you before this moment, Iolaynah," said a voice behind her.

Droman Grigso stepped from the shadows of the dungeon's entrance, shrugging off his fine robes. Flanking his shoulders at sharp angles was an iron-fused armor. Fists closed at the breastbone, and where there should have been shoulder plates, tiny skulls formed hard epaulettes, and a matching skull glared straight ahead at the point of a molded helmet attached to the shoulder piece, transforming Droman Grigso into an iron beast uprooted from the poisonous soils of the Deep Hells.

Iolaynah swallowed. "How do you know me? Why was Lorameere invited here?"

A low, menacing laugh trickled from Grigso's mouth, and Iolaynah suddenly realized how eerily silent the echoing dungeon had become. Grigso's presence had the ability to snuff out even the sounds of death.

"With your hand on the hilt of your father's bone dagger, you still ask such questions," he mocked.

Iolaynah's thumb traced the jeweled hilt that had imbued her with her father's strength after so many years of needing him, of aching at the memory of his funeral.

"*Bone* dagger?" she whispered.

Iolaynah unsheathed her weapon, which brought a ghoulish smile to his lips.

"He never told you what he was," Grigso whispered.

"H-he never told me—" Iolaynah stumbled. It couldn't be true.

Except she knew it was. In a deep, unreachable place inside of her, she had always known what he was. What *she* was.

"Your father, you, me, we're the same," Droman Grigso said, his voice soft through his hollow smile.

The word hung unspoken between them: *necromancer.*

"My father was nothing like you, and neither am I," she spat. "This is not what the Priests of Rathma taught," she cried, her voice breaking as she looked upon the room. "They bring Balance to Sanctuary. Life *and* death. What is it *you* bring? Chaos? *Suffering?*"

Grigso's smile fell, and he slowly shook his head. "You continue to disappoint," he said, then turned to the murky dungeon entrance. "Your Lorameere figured it out long ago."

Iolaynah's heart squeezed as a pale, bent Lorameere emerged from the shadows.

Iolaynah lunged for her sister, but Grigso withdrew a long scythe from behind his back, slicing it through the air between them, missing Iolaynah with the tip of its crescent by inches.

Lorameere's gaze never left the ground. Her once dewy skin cracked, and her bones jutted at sharp angles. She swayed slowly in place, and when Iolaynah looked at her feet, she understood it was because her body was nearly petrified from the knees down.

The husked remains lining the walls. The trophy in the middle of the room with its tortured faces. The slow death that permeated the sanctum.

Iolaynah looked up at Droman Grigso, barely able to say the words: "You're life-tapping these people."

Grigso lowered his scythe and took a step toward Iolaynah, but she raised her bone dagger, and he held his hands up in a mock show of truce.

"Tell me, girl," he baited her, "for all your supposed devotion to the Balance, what have you ever done to serve it? Had you known you possessed necromantic gifts, would you have raised the dead in service to your precious Balance? Your father—what of his contribution? Would you like to know what Lorameere would have done?"

Iolaynah flinched.

"She would have reanimated your father." Grigso smiled at her, clearly savoring Iolaynah's confusion. "Ah yes, returned to that pit in the oil sands. All to see you smile again. To be a family again . . . no matter how twisted."

Iolaynah glared at Grigso. "She never would have wanted that if she'd known the cost."

Grigso suddenly struck the butt of his scythe on the stone floor. "I tire of your self-righteousness, girl. I'd held some hope you might be among one of the promising students I used to reanimate in the early times."

Iolaynah looked again to the morbid trophy on the pedestal behind her.

"Theirs were the brightest minds to pass through these halls. I knew that if any lives could add back the years stolen from me, it would be theirs. Alas, their bodies eventually failed too."

Iolaynah gazed upon the rows of husks, the half-living creatures tangled in roots . . . her nearly lost Lorameere.

"You had no right." She choked back tears.

"*They* had no right," Grigso bellowed, his voice crackling through the dungeon. "The Priests of Rathma would curse me with such knowledge only to damn me with this horrid sickness! I tell you this: no student who has crossed the threshold of this sanctum has ever borne the agony I bear, but I'll make sure you suffer your share of it before I take your life."

With thunderous force, Grigso swung his scythe into the wall, sinking it into one of the living roots snaking its way through the husks. Once pierced, the root reached for Lorameere.

"Look out!" Iolaynah screamed, lunging, but as she did, the row of corpses restrained by the roots fell forward, reanimated by the strike of Grigso's scythe.

Tearing at her with their cracked, rotted nails, the petrified bodies scraped and bit at Iolaynah, overcoming her before she could take a single swing. She could feel the twist of each joint, the pull of each muscle. Then came the crushing weight, dozens of bodies piling atop her as they squeezed the air from Iolaynah's lungs. Through a space in the bodies, she could see a writhing Lorameere's last ounces of life draining from her body as the root gripped tighter, all while Droman Grigso looked on.

Behind him, a quivering Elden crouched in the shadows.

Grigso doesn't see him.

There's still a chance, Iolaynah thought. She heard crackling, felt the agonizing *pop* of her ribs breaking under the weight of flailing dead bodies. Her vision began to fade . . .

If she'd just waited for me. *That's what Elden had said. There's still a chance. Help Lorameere, Elden. Please, I can't—*

The Kehjistani sun was hot on Iolaynah's face. The smell of her father was cedarwood and tobacco.

"You've grown," he said, his voice rich and real in her ear. "You handle the dagger well. The sapphire eye follows you. It knows you're now its owner."

Iolaynah stared at the hilt of the dagger. "I wish it still belonged to you," she said sadly, wiping the tear trickling down her cheek.

"It was my time," he said. "The Balance required it."

TEARING AT HER
WITH THEIR CRACKED,
ROTTED NAILS, THE
PETRIFIED BODIES

SCRAPED AND BIT AT
IOLAYNAH, OVERCOMING
HER BEFORE SHE COULD
TAKE A SINGLE SWING.

"Why did you never tell me?" she asked him without looking up. She feared if she did, he would no longer be there.

He was quiet for a while. Then, slowly, he said, "Sometimes, we must learn in our own way. Sometimes, we must learn with pain."

Iolaynah considered his answer. "Why?"

"Pain teaches us what matters most."

Iolaynah shook her head. "But what if . . . those who truly mattered to me are lost? When does the pain cease?"

Her father did not answer. When she looked up, she was alone.

Iolaynah gasped awake, but the claws of death kept her firmly on the dungeon floor.

"There, there, girl," Droman Grigso cooed, his rank breath warm on her face.

She tried to recoil from him, but every muscle in Iolaynah's body screamed in agony. The headmaster's army of corpses had receded. The thorny roots slithering from the wall's crevices were winding and piercing deep, bloody grooves into her skin, leaving her too weak to stand.

"That's it. Calm yourself. Let it heal you," his voice wafted. "This is how you were destined to use your power, Iolaynah."

When her eyes regained their focus, it was upon a green silk ribbon lying beside her. Iolaynah stared at it for several long seconds before she recognized the brittle black hair tangled through it, cupped in her twitching hand. Curled into a *C* facing her was her dearest Lorameere, the same root binding them, pulling the last drops of life from Lorameere to bring Iolaynah back to life.

"Please, make it stop," Lorameere begged, one last tear trickling down her withering face.

"Grigso, I give my life for hers!" Iolaynah pleaded, but Grigso slammed his fists upon the trophy pedestal.

"If you're still too stubborn to see your greater potential, then you deserve to die alongside her!"

My dagger. If only I could reach my dagger to cut away the roots, thought Iolaynah. But the bindings were too tight. The light was nearly gone from Lorameere's eyes.

Suddenly, a feral, unearthly scream echoed through the dungeon, and a sickening *squelch* filled the air.

"What have you done?" Iolaynah heard Grigso yell.

The roots around her arms loosened, and she heard the *clink* of her dagger land on the ground beneath her. Iolaynah wriggled her hand to the hilt and grasped it hard, sawing frantically, feeling sap smear over her as she freed herself. Just as she moved to free Lorameere, she saw Grigso shove Elden away from the scythe he'd wrenched into the source of the roots.

"Iolaynah!" Elden screamed, and she ducked as the scythe swung inches above her head.

WEAVING THE ONCE-
SILKY BLACK HAIR INTO
A LOOSE BRAID, IOLAYNAH
TIED THE GREEN RIBBON

TO THE END,
PLACING IT GENTLY
OVER LORAMEERE'S
SHOULDER.

Tumbling to the opposite side of Grigso, Iolaynah faced off against the headmaster, her dagger like a toy against his armor and bladed staff.

"How does it feel, Iolaynah, to have your dear Lorameere's lifeblood running through your veins?"

But there was someone else's blood running through Iolaynah, whose blood was never poisoned by Droman Grigso and his betrayal of the Balance or the teachings of Rathma.

"She joins my father's blood," Iolaynah said, gripping the bone dagger in her fist. "And with it, I will restore the Balance you have desecrated."

Iolaynah slashed her dagger at the binding root holding the nearest wall of corpses in place. Grigso stumbled back as if struck. In that moment, Iolaynah aimed the sharp blade tip straight between the closed fists at his armor's heart. With a *crack*, she felt her dagger pierce the iron, slipping between Grigso's ribs to his soft insides.

A hideous cry escaped him then, and as she bore down and twisted her blade deeper, she leaned close to his face, enjoying the first glimmer of fear in his eyes.

"How does it feel?" she raged, teeth clenched, "as the lives you stole drain from your body?"

Even through his agony, Grigso smiled, his mouth filling with blood. "I gave them new life through me. Don't you see? *We* are what the Priests of Rathma fear most—not guardians, but deciders of the Balance."

Grigso winced as his face and hands wrinkled to their true age. Still, he spoke:

"It is not too late for you, Iolaynah. Think of your father and sister, of all the great minds you could rebirth in this world. Surely they deserve a second chance."

Droman Grigso's eyes fluttered, and he sputtered a last bloody cough before grasping Iolaynah's hand over the hilt of her dagger.

Choking, he whispered, "Dear Iolaynah. I've made a student of you yet. Oh, how painful such a truth must be to you."

With this last swipe at her heart, Droman Grigso plunged the dagger straight through, carrying Iolaynah's hands with it, pulling the hilt deep inside the hot cavity of his own chest until she felt the blade puncture the ground underneath.

Droman Grigso was dead.

Her hands still dripping with Grigso's blood, Iolaynah walked slowly to the limp body of her sweet Lorameere. Elden lay beside her, his tiny body trembling with silent tears. She was his reason for living too.

Weaving the once-silky black hair into a loose braid, Iolaynah tied the green ribbon to the end, placing it gently over Lorameere's shoulder.

She pressed her cheek to Lorameere's, her sister already cold to the touch, but she let the tears flow while she cursed the High Heavens.

"Why her? Why would you take her? If there is a Balance and

I'm meant to keep it, why would you take everyone who ties me to it?"

She wept until night turned to day and turned again to night, then kissed Lorameere once more on her cold forehead.

"You were my very last tether," she whispered to her sister, then turned to Elden, who had not moved from Lorameere's side.

"Bury her in the light," Iolaynah said.

The harness slipped easily from Droman Grigso's limp shoulders, and the helmet rested heavily on her head. Iolaynah would need them to hold her firmly to the ground as she walked alone through the doors of the sanctum and toward the shore of the Twin Seas.

It was Iolaynah, the girl from Kehjistan, who seized on Droman Grigso's moment of weakness and drove her father's bone dagger blade through his heart. Aware of her latent powers for mere minutes and barely alive with only the lifeblood of her sister to keep her standing, Iolaynah silenced the screams emanating from the sanctum at the edge of the Scosglen moors once and for all. But her win was far from victorious, for every anchor that had once held her in place—her beloved sister, the truth of her father, her belief in the Balance—was no more.

Cursed to walk the remainder of her days with the blood of her sister flowing through her veins, those who dared to get close enough spoke of a warrior who woke nightly from tortured dreams and performed endless acts of unanswered penance. She gripped the hilt of her fabled bone dagger with every exhale, its jeweled tip always staring up at her. Unpracticed at speaking, she grew nearly wordless over the years, choosing instead to watch, allowing a cloak of dark silence to settle upon her shoulders as heavily as the armor she refused to remove, the skulls staring into nothingness as Iolaynah bore her gaze into the soul of anyone studying her own countenance for long enough.

Her anchors' chains severed, it is said that Iolaynah was forever after unmoored.

I, Tejal, see the warrior in my dreams, a girl who sometimes ages, sometimes remains the young woman who first set upon the sanctum to unveil Droman Grigso for the rogue he was. In my visions, she is a fearsome sister, a terrified orphan, a bloodied and battered soldier for the Balance, a solitary wanderer. She is a necromancer. She is Iolaynah, who dons the armor forged from the Sanctum of Bone.

Teeth of the Plague

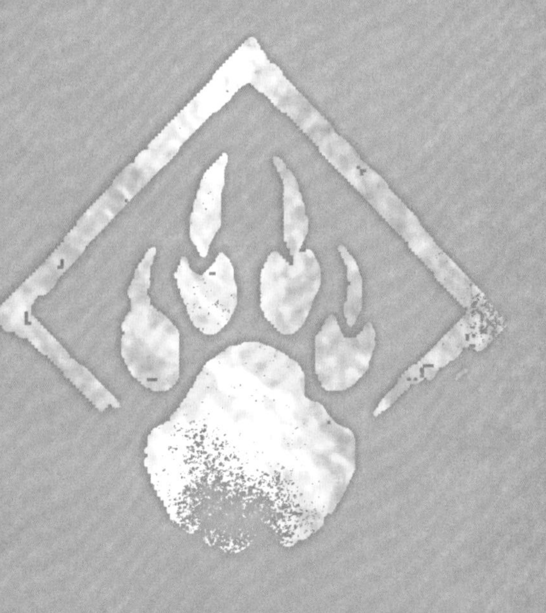

A SHORT STORY BY

Z BREWER

TEETH OF THE PLAGUE

This tale speaks of two legends. One born of the wilds . . . and one born within city walls.

I, Tejal, have served as witness to both in visions that haunt me to this very day. Gather yourself now and listen as I regale you with a story about a young druid boy . . . and the thing that he will become.

A plague has stretched its shadow hand across the map, finally reaching a small city not far from Westmarch. The people look to their lord to ease their suffering, but their cries fall on willfully closed ears. Even now, I can hear the whispered rumors of the plague's origin—whispers that will fuel the flames and forever scorch the city.

We begin with a conversation—and we end in blood . . .

"My lord," Holps said, wringing his hands, "food is already scarce. The peasants may revolt at such an order. If you damn the peasants, our crops will lie untended in the fields—"

The lord scoffed. "Now I need care what the filthy underclass has to say? I am their *lord. Your* lord. See that my will is done."

Another man, Ardan, cleared his throat—its sound echoing off the chamber walls. "Forgive me, sire, b-but your people are starving. Please, might you reconsider—"

Kirek could see their pleas would lead nowhere. There were more urgent matters to which to attend, and little time to waste. "Sire. Urgent tidings from Westmarch." As he addressed his lord, he noticed movement to his right. Through the wall, between a gap in the barnstones, Kirek spied the young druid boy, Vylum, whom his lordship had taken in as a babe. Vylum had always made Kirek uneasy. He saw too much and said too little, creeping about the castle like an uninvited guest. For company, he shunned the children his age in favor of the castle rats. Even now, the boy stared at him with eyes that made no promise of a soul within, nuzzling the rat on his shoulder as it nibbled the fabric of his finespun tunic.

The lord grumbled dismissively. "What now? More news about this peasant rebellion?"

"Sire. It is a problem far more grave. A great disease, spreading quickly. We have reports of thousands dying in the streets: boils on their skin, splitting open with pus. It seems to have reached the holdfast as well." Kirek swallowed hard, looked back over his shoulder, and signaled to the guard who stood out in the hall. "It appears a plague has come to our lands, my liege."

The guard, hands gloved and mouth covered by a cloth, dragged someone into the room and tossed him down before the men. Kirek's heart beat faster with fear. He didn't know how the lord would react. He only knew that his lordship would do nothing unless he saw proof with his own eyes, and now that proof was kneeling before him, coughing and quivering.

The lord sat back on his throne, his brow furrowed. The peasant coughed and, with spittle still dangling from his lips, moaned in pain. His face and arms were covered in boils—several of which had burst open, leaving a greasy sheen on his already filth-covered skin.

Kirek spoke again, his voice softer. "The apothecaries say hordes of rats are spreading the sickness like wildfire. But the lowborn say it is perhaps the curse of . . . a druid."

The lord shook his head. "A curse indeed, but no druid caused this. The druids are friends to this holdfast, and to your lord. Be mindful where you place blame, Kirek. Or have you forgotten my son was once counted among their kind? If not for the druids, I'd have no heir at all."

Kirek's mind turned to the boy watching within the walls. He wondered if Vylum had any idea of his true parentage. If the lad did not know before, he certainly did now. A fitting reward for his lurking and eavesdropping.

Kirek addressed the lord once more. "Your son beckons rats inside the castle walls, sire, makes them fat on food that could better fill the bellies of your starving subjects."

"Rats seldom starve," Vylum said now, his voice loud enough to carry. "Deny them the crumbs from your meal and they might make a meal of you instead." He looked at Kirek with dark eyes, a smile full of crooked teeth.

Kirek continued, ignoring the outburst. "Druidic curse or not, your son is contributing to this plague. The apothecaries advise we smoke out these creatures and burn them—"

"Mind your tongue, Kirek. Lest I order it removed." There was the briefest of pauses as the lord's gaze shifted from Kirek back to the messages lying on the table before him, awaiting his attention. "Perhaps we can settle two problems with the same solution: take no action. Let the lowborn starve and fester, believing themselves cursed. Their deaths will save food and slow the plague. You have your orders."

Kirek looked to his comrades Holps and Ardan for help, only to discover their expressions had hardened. All hope of saving the people had dissipated at his lordship's words. The only ones who looked pleased were the lord and his son, who seemed content that his rat friends would face no harm in the coming days.

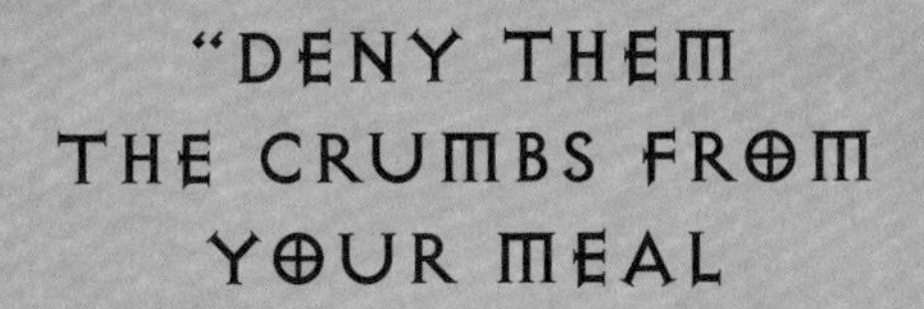

"DENY THEM
THE CRUMBS FROM
YOUR MEAL

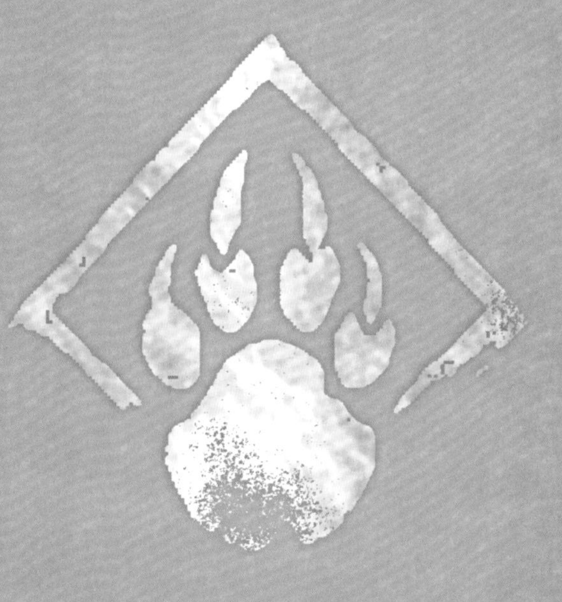

AND THEY MIGHT
MAKE A MEAL OF
YOU INSTEAD."

Months passed.

The wave of death and ill fortune had become known as the Great Pestilence. It swept through Westmarch, taking the life of even the lord. Soon, barely half their number remained. At the behest of the surviving citizens, Kirek, Holps, and Ardan took on the harrowing task of leadership. They followed the apothecaries' advice and took to caring for the lowest among them, even clearing the plague-ridden corpses within the city walls.

As Kirek hoisted another body over his shoulder like a sack of grain, he tried hard not to inhale. The stench of rotting flesh and open boils had turned his stomach enough in recent days, and while he was determined to help the city, the smell of death and decay was almost too much to bear. There were no funerals—only burn piles. That is, all but for his lordship. In the end, the lord had died gasping and coughing, and it had been Kirek who'd placed his lifeless body within the grave that Holps and Ardan had dug. They'd have buried his druid son as well, but the boy must have fled the holdfast for safer lands or died in some crevice of the castle, unbeknownst to them. *Good riddance,* Kirek thought as he dropped the body he'd been carrying onto the burn pile and collected another.

Holps tilted his head to the side as he examined the limp form hanging over Kirek's shoulder. "Are we sure this one's dead?"

Kirek tilted the body forward to examine the face, a mask of pockmarks crusted with infection and green pus.

As Kirek's eyes fell on the corpse's face, his lips curled in disgust.

"It's *him*. The druid boy. Like father, like son—as worthless in death as in life, I say. Better we get to the burning."

The corner of Vylum's mouth twitched—those same sharp teeth forming a smile, even so near to death.

Ardan gasped. "He's alive!"

Kirek could summon no pity. "The boy's beloved rats—a remnant of his filthy druidic parentage—hastened this plague, I am certain. Let him die and help put an end to it." Then Kirek spoke to Vylum, who seemed oddly at ease in the plague's grip. "Are you done with the misery of your existence, boy? Because the rest of us are."

And with that, Kirek dropped Vylum's limp, gnarled form onto the burn pile, which hissed in a gasp of smoke and fresh flames.

Cruel laughter boiled out of the three men as they walked away, joined by the crackling of the flames. Kirek gave one last glance back, watching a fresh layer of sweat glistening on Vylum's brow as the heat of the fires spread closer. Ever closer.

He waited until the flames lapped at the lad's skin, sizzling his sweat, before turning away.

Years passed.

The Great Pestilence lasted all that time. When it finally came to an end, Kirek, Ardan, and Holps found themselves with a wealth and power they had only ever imagined. Their sprawling pastoral estates were well kept and idyllic, with the lowborn eager to repay the service each man had given in plague time, and they knew neither toil nor hardship. After hailing them as heroes, their new lord assigned them one final duty: overseeing the removal of all vermin within the city. For while the plague had passed, the rats remained, consuming stores of grain and threatening to spread sickness anew. Worse, they had been acting strange, excitable, as if something they had been long awaiting would soon come to pass. Peasants even claimed to have seen the rats moving as one large mass through the alleyways at night . . .

"I thought we'd given enough of our time to cleaning up this damned plague, yet here we are again, trudging through the sewers like the very rats we're hunting." Kirek shone his torch down the darkened tunnel, searching for signs of infestation. In his free hand, a sack full of captured vermin floated on the water, fighting his attempts to drown them. Ardan carried his own bag filled with rodents—dead from ingesting a poison the apothecaries had concocted. When they arrived back at the sewer entrance, they would add the vermin to the burn pile. "And where in the name of all the Hells has Holps run off to? Not like him to shirk his duties."

"Probably home, drinking his cellar dry. I envy him." Ardan cast a glance around them, taking in the grimy stone walls of the sewer. "This place makes me uneasy. It feels like, like *we're* the ones being hunted . . ."

Kirek nodded in agreement. He hadn't felt right ever since they'd entered. There were eyes on him, thousands of eyes he couldn't see, though he felt their weight nonetheless. "Let's take our leave and join Holps. The sooner we're away from this stench, the better."

But when they reached Holps's manor, they found the front door standing ajar. Furniture had been tossed about, splintered, and perhaps gnawed on. The fireplace was filled with softly dying embers. A trail of black sludge soiled the fine carpets of his sitting room; they followed it to his chambers and into his featherbed. The bed was empty, save for a large rat's skull carved with runes they did not recognize or understand.

No doubt lingered in their minds. Holps was missing.

And something in the sewers had taken him.

Ardan held up a mug to toast, his words slurring. "To our absent friend."

The tavern they sat in had no name, but it had good ale and decent food and, most importantly, an air of anonymity. Ale slopped from fresh mugs as the barmaid set them on the counter, but neither Kirek nor Ardan noticed. Truth was, they were six drinks each into debating what had happened to Holps, and no amount of ale would ever be enough to wipe from their memories what they'd seen. Kirek turned the rat's skull over and over in his hand, studying it in the glow of the crackling fireplace.

Then Kirek lifted his mug, clanking it against Ardan's.

The barmaid ran a cloth over the countertop. "So, how did he die?"

"Never said he died." Kirek tossed his head back, swallowing mouthfuls of ale before wiping his mouth clean with the back of his hand. "He's *missing*."

Clucking her tongue, the barmaid shook her head. "A shame. But not the first to go missing 'round these parts of late."

Ardan's voice shook just as much as the mug in his hand. "That's no ordinary rat's skull, Kirek. The size of the damn thing . . . must be from a plagued vermin. Hear those things are the size of cats. And those runes . . . they look druidic. You don't think—"

"Keep it together, mate." Kirek glanced around nervously.

The barmaid straightened some. "Druidic runes, you say?"

Kirek grumbled, wishing she would mind her business. "Yes. What of it?"

"It's probably nothing, but I've been hearing stories about a creature said to have the soul of a thousand vermin." Wiping off her hands on her apron, the barmaid leaned in, holding the men's attention as she spoke. "He wears a worn disc carved with runes on a string around his neck. Some say that it acts as a beacon, aiding him in his murderous endeavors. He snatches folk into the sewers, where he and his pack of rats feast on their brains and eyes."

The men fell silent for some time, until at last Kirek scoffed. "Ludicrous. Holps likely won a hand of cards and pissed off the wrong man."

Ardan gulped. "Think there's something . . . *unearthly* lurking in the sewers?"

The barmaid's eyes gleamed. "I'm sure it's just rumors. Your friend'll turn up soon."

Hours passed.

The moon hung full and low in the sky, casting a cool blue tint over the thatched rooftops and cobblestoned streets. On any other evening, it would have been a welcome sight, but this night was filled with too many shadows for Kirek. All he could think about as he staggered home was the look in the barmaid's eyes as she spoke of the creature who dwelled in the sewers. It had sent a strange chill up his spine—one that lingered.

Kirek ambled from street to street, his missing friend consuming his every thought. As he emerged from an alley, he noticed several rats gathered in the street before him.

"Ah, here you are." He kicked the first one into a wall; a moist, satisfying *thump* accompanied its final squeal. He stomped on the next, grinding the rodent's skull into the cobblestones. With each tiny death, he felt a bit of twisted pleasure.

Across the street, a dark entrance to the sewers caught his attention. He couldn't shake the feeling he was being watched from its gaping maw. But by whom? And was he seeing things, or were there two glowing green pinpricks of eyes in the dark? He blinked, and they were gone.

"Good riddance, filth," he slurred.

Moments later, he was stepping foot inside his home, content to pass out in his bed next to his wife. The last thought he had before his head hit the pillow was of Holps and the rat skull.

And the glowing green pinpricks of eyes.

A day passed.

The door to Ardan's home stood open as Kirek approached, reminding him too much of the way he and Ardan had found Holps's place the day before. As he moved slowly through the dark house, he winced at the tacky sound his boots made upon the stone floor, not knowing what it was and somewhat afraid to light a candle and remove all doubt. But as he proceeded to the back of the house, he noticed his boots were now splashing black sludge about with each step.

Still, he pressed on. Where were Ardan and his wife? Despite his fears, he located a candlestick in the dark and lit it with the tinderbox from his pocket. Turning slowly, he surveyed the room, then stopped, bile rising in his throat.

Two figures were tied to the bed, each stripped of every bit of skin and muscle and tissue. Ardan. Cassandra. The blankets were drenched in blood and bodily fluids—so much so that the fabric couldn't hold it all, the gristle and blood dripping onto the floor. On the bed between the corpses was an oversize rat skull, carved with runes. Just like the one they'd found at Holps's home.

Kirek vomited before bolting out of the house, his heart rattling inside his chest, pounding like fists against his rib cage. He needed to run. He needed to keep moving. He needed to get home. This, paired with the disappearance of Holps the day before—Kirek now knew that he and his family were no longer safe in the city.

He raced through the shadows, but the scuffling sound behind him was distracting. Casting glances over his shoulder, he saw no one following, but the sensation of eyes boring into his back refused to leave him. Panic filled his every breath. How could he go home? If this thing followed him there . . .

Forcing from his mind the gruesome image of Ardan and Cassandra, Kirek quickened his steps through the streets. Who had slain Ardan and his wife, and in such a horrific way? Had it been the city guard, at the behest of their new lord? Perhaps their new liege—a wise but mercurial man—was displeased with their failed attempts to quell the rodent infestation and had run out of patience with them. But to resort to *execution*? And if not him, then who?

Or *what?*

A creature said to have the soul of a thousand vermin . . .

Ducking into a sewer opening, Kirek debated staying there until he was certain his pursuer was gone—that is, if he *was* being

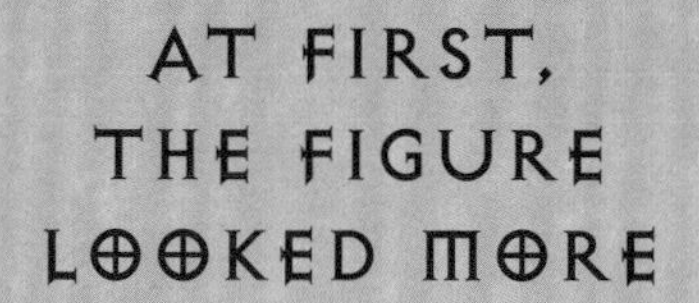

AT FIRST,
THE FIGURE
LOOKED MORE

MORE LIKE AN
AMALGAMATION
OF RODENTS
THAN A MAN.

pursued. Then he recalled there was a route home through the sewers. Without thinking, he vanished into the dark waterways, groping the slimy walls.

After a while of stumbling through the tunnels, he came to rest in an open chamber. Roots had twisted through the stone above, forming cracks that let in a few pale streaks of moonlight. He figured he must be under the tree-filled town square.

He wondered if those above would be able to hear him, should he scream. Before him, bits of bone dangled from strings on the ceiling, clinking together like ghastly wind chimes. Clay pots in various sizes cluttered the space—some home to plants, others to a wide variety of fungi. An old wagon wheel sat propped against one wall, serving as a trellis to a climbing vine. A bed in the corner lay heaped with rotten animal skins, blanketing the space in a thick odor.

At the center of the room sat a bubbling pot, tiny animal skulls floating on the surface.

His heart pounded as he spun around, looking for the way back out, eyes falling on a human skull protruding from a garden and a rash of mushrooms winding up the rough-hewn wall. A low, rumbling laugh drew his attention to the far side of the room.

At first, the figure looked more like an amalgamation of rodents than a man. But then Kirek could see that this cloaked figure was indeed human, wearing layers of pelts, his face obscured by a hood and mask. There were bones—skulls—tied with strips of cloth and string around his neck, and at his hip, and on his boot. And were those rat corpses strung over one of his broad shoulders?

"Please. I didn't mean to—I'd just like to leave," Kirek managed.

The figure laughed again, pulling down his hood and mask to reveal a bald head painted with tattoos. Still, something about him seemed familiar. The sharp teeth of his mouth as it split into a smile.

Recognition washed over Kirek, and he could see the boy this man had once been. Kirek cleared his throat. "You're the . . . the old lord's adopted ward. You're—you're a-alive. V-Vylum, isn't it?"

"It *was*." His words shifted into a peculiar chuckle as a large black rat took its perch on his shoulder. As the rat sniffed at Vylum's mouth, it looked almost like the creature was giving him a kiss. "But I am so much more than that now."

Something heavy settled at the bottom of Kirek's gut. He couldn't say for certain that Vylum was the person who'd been following him. He only knew that every bone in his body screamed to leave.

A creature said to have the soul of a thousand vermin . . .

Kirek remained frozen in place. "Why do you dwell here and not in the light of day? The holdfast—"

"The *holdfast* is a blight on the land." Vylum's voice was like ice. "This city cleared the forests for farms and marred the land with waste. It poisoned the air with smoke and choked the rivers with filth. And now, my friends are going to take back the land that mankind stole from them."

Kirek shook his head. He didn't understand. He needed to *think*, to distract the man. Gesturing to the smudged tattoos on Vylum's skin, he said, "Those marks. You didn't have them when your father was alive. W-what are they?"

"They tell my story, growing up in the sewers. I painted them myself." He grinned. He stroked a series of long rat tails hanging from his shoulder and tapped the rodent skulls and corpses above them. "These are my family members, found dead, now reunited with their great protector. And these . . ."

He passed a hand over the long, pointed bones dangling from his hip. "These are trophies, of a sort. They mark each kill. I possess only a few now, though I've many more to find. These four are new. Care to admire them?" He lifted a bone. "This one called you *husband*."

"My . . . wife. You—" The weight of grief unmoored him. The world seemed to spin, weighing him down until Kirek fell to his knees. His wife was dead. Probably murdered much in the same way as Ardan's had been.

"I-I see how I have wronged you, druid." He felt the words tumbling from his mouth faster than he could think them. "I apologize, but you need not kill me—"

"I will be the judge of that. And the rats my jury and executioners." His jaw tightened and his eyes became fiery slits as he took a step toward the weeping man. "You left me for dead."

"I said I was sorry! *Please!*"

Vylum clucked his tongue. "The rats showed me more kindness than any man ever has. After you cast me into the fire, the rats saved me, dragged me from the mound of corpses. Over the years, they've become my eyes and ears in exchange for my protection and aid. They are my only friends. They were *always* my only friends." He shook his head. "The plague was never the problem. It was the people."

Kirek tried but couldn't bear to bring himself to stand. All he could think about were his wife and comrades and how much they must have suffered in the end. Needlessly. Hot tears drew lines down his face. "Please! I am begging you, druid. Let me go! Or at least finish me quickly."

"Answer me this." Vylum locked eyes with Kirek. "Are you done with the misery of your existence?"

Kirek let out a gut-wrenching wail.

Vylum touched something that hung around his neck. A talisman, perhaps? His lips moved, but the whispers that reached Kirek's ears were coming from others. A thousand voices speaking words that Kirek could not translate. But he understood with great clarity the deadly intent of those words.

Not a talisman. No. *A beacon.*

Rats poured in through every crevice imaginable, covering the floor, surrounding Kirek in a deadly embrace, filling his ears with deafening squeaks and the endless scratching of claws scrabbling against stone, splashing through puddles and damp.

"THE RATS SHOWED ME MORE KINDNESS

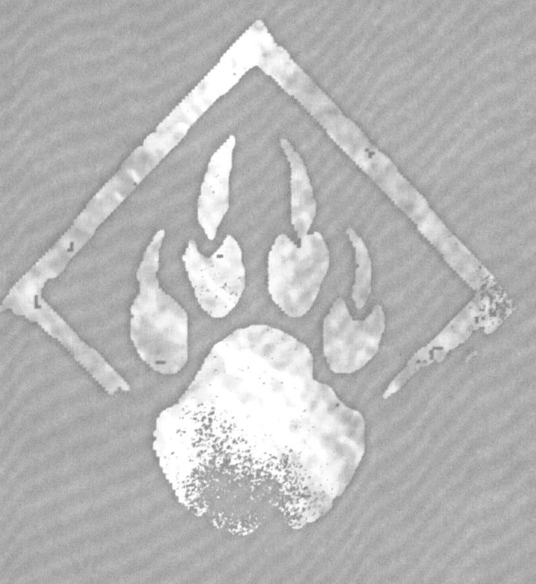

THAN ANY MAN EVER HAS."

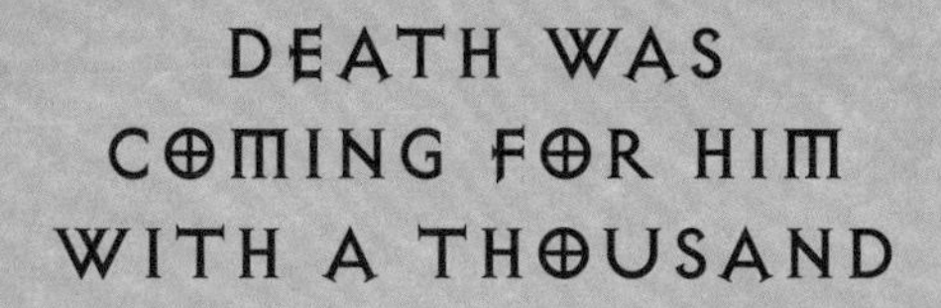

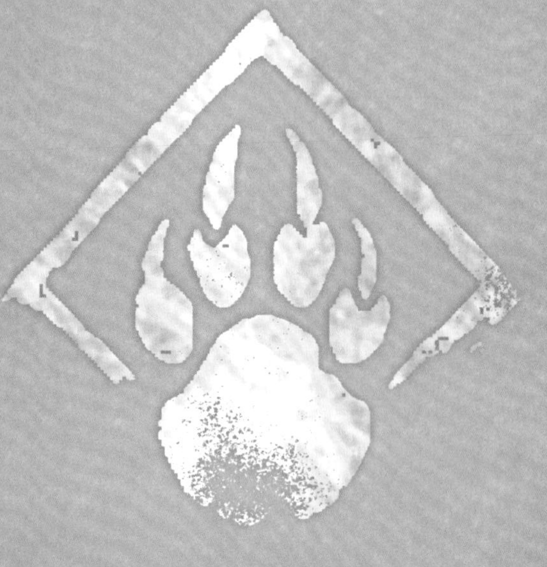

HUNGRY MOUTHS
AND THE COMMAND
OF A WHISPER.

Vylum gripped Kirek by the hair, dragged him through the mound of rats, and slammed him hard against the wall. He spoke strange words to the vermin. Commands, perhaps? Then the rats carried him on their backs as they began to flood out of the room toward the tunnel's exit.

Above, at the entrance to the sewers, was the last burn pile in the city: the one Kirek and his comrades had used to dispose of the city's rats. It was there the creatures let go of a screaming, writhing Kirek. Vylum gripped the nobleman and tossed him with surprising strength onto the burn pile.

"No!" Kirek shrieked. He reached out but could only manage to grip one of the carved bones hanging from Vylum's neck. Pain seared across Kirek's skin as he caught fire. His body was so battered that he couldn't fight back, even as the flames charred his flesh.

Death was coming for him with a thousand hungry mouths and the command of a whisper.

I, Tejal, bore witness to this vision and shall carry it with me for all my days. It is my burden. It is my gift. And it is my duty to share word of such legends to all who may listen.

No longer do rats plague the land. No longer are whispers shared there of druidic curses and a creature lurking in the dark. The people are safe.

But to this day, if you were to visit, you might catch yourself glancing over your shoulder as you walk the streets at night and keeping a close eye on shadowy corners. For the stains of blood never truly wash away.

Vylum was not the hero of this tale, nor was he its villain. At his core, he was just a boy whose soul had been crushed by this world and who sought to unleash the torment he'd experienced on those who'd caused his pain. So too could be said of Kirek, whose own suffering he'd caused himself. The world is not made of heroes and villains. Rather, it's made of people and pain and loss. What matters is what those people do with that pain and how they recover from that loss that shows us they are the stuff of legends—be it hero or villain.

May the flames of this tale singe away intruders, to allow the land to reclaim what was stolen from her . . .

The Toll of Darkness and Light

A SHORT STORY BY
JONATHAN MABERRY

THE TOLL OF DARKNESS AND LIGHT

There are stories of him. Of Klath-Ulna, called the Golden One, though in every tale he is bathed in crimson, in the blood of any who stand against him.

I, Tejal, have seen him in dreams. To the Sharval Wilds, to a small town called Saint's Calling, he came.

If you have not heard of that place, then listen, for I will tell you why. Build the fire bright, lock the door, and lean in and listen, for even as I recall that story, I can hear the toll of a holy bell hung in a belfry that was the highest point in the town. That bell was brought from Kurast to that town, and the people rejoiced, for it was blessed by the Light.

That is what they said of it. But the very wise know that talismans are seldom shields. Rather, they are symbols of hope. And on the gulf between faith and fact hangs our tale. I will tell you the truth—the dark truth—of what happened when Klath-Ulna came in answer to its call . . .

"Is that the best you can do?"

The young man stood with his legs wide, weight shifted to the balls of his feet, knees bent and springy. He had a broad-bladed short sword in one hand and a small buckler strapped over his other hand and wrist. Sweat glistened on his naked chest and shoulders and ran in lines down his face.

"I thought warhogs were fierce," he taunted. "Come and get me if you can, and I'll fill hell with you and—"

"Really?" said the old man who leaned on the handle of the sparring wheel. "Every time, Jenks? Except this time, warhogs? What in the name of all that's holy are warhogs? Did you mean *wart*hogs? Because we don't have them anywhere near here."

"Come on, Bikleman. You're not doing this right." Jenks straightened. "*War*hogs! Don't you listen to *any* of the old songs?"

"What's a warhog, then? A hog with a hatchet? Sow with a sword?"

"They were demons from—"

"No," interrupted Bikleman sharply. "We're not doing that. You're too old to be making things up. Besides, there are enough *real* monsters in the world to worry about without demons."

"But—"

"But nothing," growled Bikleman. "It was long ago that demons walked abroad. You risk conjuring them up from all your talk of them! You should focus on what you might *actually* need to fight one day."

"What? *People?* That's so boring."

"Boring? *Boring*, is it now?" cried the old man, rolling his eyes and shaking his head. "You tell everyone you want to be a paladin, a soldier of the Light, a champion of the Zakarum faith. You were too sickly as a child to enter training, and now that you're older and fit, I would have thought you could at least *try* to be serious. This is important training, Jenks. You are training to fight soldiers and brigands, thieves, and highwaymen. Those are the real threats, and if they come riding into town, then you need to be ready. Or is that too much to ask?"

Jenks, who was seventeen and had never been farther from town than Ferryman's Creek, felt his cheeks grow red. "I *am* serious."

"Then act it. Demons you make up or those you borrow from bedtime stories are nothing but distractions. If you'd take time to read the history scrolls, then you'd understand. A paladin needs to be practical. Realistic. The stuff you're supposed to be reading is in the books of holy learning, but I don't suppose you've even *read* them."

"I . . . read them," said Jenks defensively. Then he mumbled. "Mostly."

"Uh-huh." The old man gave the training wheel a sudden shove, and the many wooden arms swung around with shocking speed.

Jenks was caught flat-footed and had to drop into a squat to evade the big top arm, then leap like a frog over the ankle-sweeper. He hit the ground and rolled, coming up as the gut-punch arm tried to smash into his belly. But Jenks twisted away, bending backward like a dancer. The smaller whipsaw arm came around faster than all the others, and Jenks checked it with his buckler and stabbed out at the heart target—a canvas pad stuffed with straw. The blunt wooden sword hit solidly, and Jenks broke out into a fierce grin of triumph.

"*Ha!*" he cried. "And the warhog demon is slain."

Bikleman kicked one of the straight rods that transfixed the wheel, and the padded end hit Jenks squarely in the crotch. The lad uttered a high, whistling shriek and dropped to his knees, his sword falling into the dust. He cupped himself and, turning a shocking shade of purple, toppled sideways.

The old man limped around and stood over him, smiling down. "Them warhogs are tricky beasts, aren't they, lad?"

Jenks tried to yell at him. He tried to curse him to the deepest pits of the Hells. He tried to say that it didn't hurt at all. He tried to get to his feet to prove he wasn't wounded.

In all of that, he failed.

Bikleman turned and spit downwind with great accuracy and velocity, hitting the heart target in the exact center.

"Good session, Jenks," he said dryly. "Maybe tomorrow you can show me how to fight an undead hedgehog or some such rot."

Jenks rolled over and vomited.

The old man looked down at him for a moment. "You're a good lad, Jenks. But you need to be a better *man*. You look at me and see an old coot, but I was a paladin once, as you well know. Long before you were born, but not so long ago that I can't remember what it feels like—in muscle and bone, in heart and mind—to cross blades with an enemy soldier. Not a monster, but a warrior trained in all the arts of killing. There is nothing more dreadful, I can assure you, than a warrior who has skill and armor, weapons and heart, and wants your blood on his or her blade. *I* remember that from when the Rakkis Crusades began. Not a night goes by that I don't dream of the clash of steel and the cries of the dying. Standing ankle-deep in the blood of my sisters and brothers. Of my friends." He shook his head. "People are monsters enough when the battle lust is upon then. We don't need to make up more."

Despite his words, his smile was kindly. "I'll see you at dinner."

The old man turned and limped back to town, whistling a battle hymn he and his lost companions had once sung as they'd marched off to war.

Jenks got up eventually, but then sat down again, his back to the central column of the training wheel. Once the enormity of the pain had diminished, he focused his mind on it, allowing it to be what it was. Pain. Agony. He forced himself to accept it as part of the price of growing into a warrior.

Bikleman limped because he had taken a spear through his hip. Old Redharn, the blacksmith, had half a dozen scars from blade and arrow. And there were plenty of others. Half the old men and women, many of whom had been soldiers gone to war filled with holy purpose. Like Redharn, they wore the scars they had earned in one battle or another, and on winter eves they would regale their friends with tales of valor and combat.

And as for the younger fighters from town . . .

Well, there was a whole generation that had never come home from the Crusades. Jenks conjured stories in his mind of how they went down bravely, fighting through their pain, battling on, even as their lifeblood drained away. Heroes all, he was sure of it.

But it was speculation. There was a huge gap in the ages of the people in town, an entire generation that had joined up to fight in the Crusades. From those only a few years younger than Bikleman to those barely a year older than Jenks. All of them, gone. None had returned. Not even the very young—the other lads and lasses who'd left school and town to go off as squires or junior pikemen or apprentice archers.

All gone.

All dead.

Their stories, alas, were unknown and untold. There were songs about them, some of which were even sung in church, but Jenks knew they were fake tales. As false as his imagined warhogs and goblins. The congregation sang ballads written by family or friends of the lost. Songs of courage and valor to gladden the heart and make the losses bearable.

Jenks knew that he would have been one of that company, but as a boy he had been sickly and weak. By the time he'd gotten through his own war with frailty and disease, the battles were over.

Now, at seventeen, Jenks ached for war. He no longer got sick, and endless hours of training, week upon week and month upon month, had made him strong. He was quick, nimble, adept with sword and lance and bow.

Only there was no one left to fight.

Sitting there, he wept for the chance to be a true warrior, to stand between some brutal harm and those he loved. It was his greatest dream, but even though he trained night and day, he knew that it was for naught.

"The war is over," he said to no one. "Maybe there will be another . . ."

Which was when the screams started.

He stood there at the edge of town. Jenks crouched behind the corner of a barn and stared at him.

Him.

It was a man, though unlike any Jenks had seen. Taller even than Big Gorf and more heavily muscled than Redharn the blacksmith. It was like seeing something from one of the old legends come to life. The stranger had massive shoulders, a deep chest, huge gauntlets, and dark eyes that seemed to exude a wintery coldness. He looked like a statue from a museum of death. Fully armored in a mix of metals both familiar and strange. Much of it was painted with real gold, though that shining metal was scored and dented from a thousand battles. His shoulder plates were broader than his already powerful shoulders, and from each rose a forest of spikes. There were likewise spikes on his elbows and along his buckler and greaves and even rising from his heavy boots. Worked into the pattern of that armor were symbols of death—skulls and bones. And was that a Zakarum symbol plated across his chest? On the few parts of his skin that were visible, namely his thick neck and bald head, Jenks saw tattoos—crude and ugly and ominous.

And his weapons.

Knives with plain handles—weapons not made for court or show. And slung over one brawny shoulder was the handle of a mace that looked too large, too heavy, for anyone to wield in a real fight. The body of the thing was shaped like a holy bell, except where the mouth of the bell should have been there was a

HE WAS QUICK, NIMBLE,
ADEPT WITH SWORD

AND LANCE
AND BOW.

cluster of dagger-sharp spikes, with two curved talon-like spikes thrusting outward from the canons and the iron ball at the end of the long handle. The very fact that this man carried a weapon of that size was frightening. It promised awful things.

The stranger—this warrior—looked down the main street of town. His gaze lingered for but a moment on the faces of people concealed behind wagons or parted curtains or half-opened doorways. Some whispered that this was a barbarian from the wastelands; others insisted it was a druid come to practice some dark magic. In either case, the people made signs of protection in the air and murmured sacred prayers.

Then his dark gaze moved up to the tall belfry of the only church in Saint's Calling. A Zakarum church bell older than the town itself, smithed and blessed in the east, and brought west during the crusade. The story was that bells like this had been left behind in many camps in the hopes that towns of the faithful would rise up around it. As Saint's Calling had. The bell in the tower was the old treasure in that poor town, but by its presence they were all rich in faith. The shadow of its tower, with the afternoon sun behind it, now fell along the center of the street so that it reached to within inches of the stranger's steel-capped boots.

He knelt slowly, touched his fingers to the shadow, and closed his eyes for a long moment. Jenks saw him take a deep breath and exhale before nodding to himself. Then the warrior rose to his full height and looked around.

"People of Saint's Calling," he said in a voice that was deep as thunder. "I am Klath-Ulna of the Bear Tribe, my people are the Children of Bul-Kathos, and I am called the Golden One."

His words echoed back and forth from one building to the next, rattling windows and scaring the birds from the trees.

"I seek a thing of great importance," he continued. "An iron bell in yon tower. Bring it to me and I will leave, and no harm will come to any here. Refuse me or stand in my way, and I will lay waste to all who live here. Every man and woman, down to the last infant. This I swear."

With that he reached up, took the handle of his battle-mace, and swung it over and down so that the spiked head bit deep into the shadow of the steeple. The impact seemed to shake the very ground. Fissures whipsawed away from it, cracking the hardpan. Jenks heard the gasps and even stifled screams from the watchful crowd.

The gasps faded into silence. No one moved. Not one person offered to fetch the bell for this barbarian. That heartened Jenks, because it made him think the whole town might band together and overwhelm this man.

The silence stretched as the barbarian looked from face to face. He grunted with mingled anger and disgust.

"Then I will take it myself," he said and took a single threatening step into the belfry's shadow. He glanced around. "Is there no champion who would stand against me? Is there not a single fighter in this town who will at least prove that there is honor here?"

"ARE YOU THE BEST
THIS TOWN CAN OFFER?"

KLATH-ULNA
DEMANDED.

He stood there, the mace held loosely in one hand.

Silence was the only answer.

Jenks saw the man's mouth first turn down in disappointment and then curl slowly upward with dark delight.

"I thought as much," he said, hefting his battle-mace. "It saddens me that there is no honor left in this land. No champions. What a pity. What stories will you tell when I have left? What lies will give you back your pride? What tall tales will you spin for travelers?"

No one came out of their home or store; none offered a challenge. None offered to fetch the bell yet, either. The moment stretched on and on.

Klath-Ulna spat into the dust.

Jenks gave a cry—sharp as a startled crow's—stumbled backward, whirled, and ran away.

Klath-Ulna did not look from side to side, even though he could feel the eyes on him. He could imagine the whispered words, the curses, the prayers. They would be the same here as in other towns.

How many were there now? He could not recall. Some were left intact, but so many were left in ashes, the ground soaked with blood, the bodies unburied and left for the scavengers. The names of those towns had long since faded. He never knew the names of the dead. They were nothing to him. Nothing at all.

This town would be no different.

The church loomed above him, and he could *feel* the bell calling to him. Wanting him to find it. Needing that.

And then a figure stepped out of the dense shadows by the big oak doors, and a splinter of sunlight struck fire from the bright steel in his hand.

Klath-Ulna slowed to a stop at the foot of the church stairs.

He had expected no one or everyone. It was like that sometimes. A town devoid of a great champion armed themselves with rusted swords, pitchforks, and scythes. This was neither of those things. Instead, a boy stood at the top of the stairs. Maybe sixteen or seventeen. Not a grown man. He wore a dented antique helmet, a shirt of rusted chain mail, mismatched greaves, and a very small buckler.

And a sword.

Klath-Ulna was amused. The sword looked like a good one. A real battle sword. Unlike the rest of his gear, the sword was clearly well cared for, sharp and oiled, but the blade showed no marks of use—no dents or notches. A new sword, then. Untested and unsullied, and in the hands of a boy.

"Are you the best this town can offer?" Klath-Ulna demanded.

As Jenks had hastily pulled on the armor, he had rehearsed what he would say. He now spoke out loud and clear, but his throat choked the words into meaningless mumbles. He swallowed hard and tried again.

"I am Jenks Grindelson," he said. "I am the protector of Saint's Calling, and you may not enter this church. You may not have our sacred bell. Go now and no harm will come to you."

Klath-Ulna stared at him for three full seconds before he threw back his head and laughed. It seemed to shake the whole world.

Sweat—cold and greasy with fear—popped out on Jenks's forehead. He could feel it run in icy lines down his back under his shirt. His hands were so slick with it that he had to keep readjusting his grip. He prayed that the terror he felt in his heart did not show on his face.

"Boy," said Klath-Ulna, pointing to the tattoos on his neck, "do you know what these are?"

Jenks did not trust himself to reply.

"They are the story of my search for other treasures like this bell. Each one tells the tale of towns like this. Zakarum towns filled with the faithful. Filled with people who believed that their *faith* would save them." He took a small step forward. "Those towns are ashes now. Those believers who sought shelter from the dark are nothing but blackened bones to be found in the ruins. The Light could not shield them."

The stone step on which he stood seemed to tilt under Jenks's feet.

"Some were towns five times as large as Saint's Calling. Some towns had a dozen or more warriors—seasoned fighters from the Crusades. I let them don their armor and receive blessings from their priests. With saint-blessed spears and swords etched with prayers and blessings did they confront me. And I tell you, boy, that it availed them not, for I am Klath-Ulna the Golden One. I slew them all, and they were true warriors."

He came closer and put one foot on the bottom step.

"And what are you? A stripling with bad armor and an unbloodied sword and not enough years to have learned to wipe your own ass, let alone stand in the line of battle." He shook his head. "No one else in this town has the stomach or the nerve to show their faces, never mind stand against me. But . . . boy . . . you have no chance. I have walked a thousand battlefields. I have waded through rivers of blood. Even with these tattoos to remind me, I can barely count the *towns* I've destroyed, or the number of people I have killed. Yet . . . I admire your spirit. I do. So I will do this to honor the courage that is striving to be born in you, lad."

Instead of explaining, the barbarian stood his mace against the wall. Then, with his eyes fixed on Jenks, he unbuckled the straps of his heavy chest plate. The armor fell, but he darted a hand with reptilian quickness and caught it, then lowered it to the ground. He unbuckled the spiked vambraces from his forearms and the greaves from his shins. He pulled off the cotton undershirt so that he stood wearing only leather trousers, shoes, and the wild and scattered tattoos.

"Now the fight is a fair one," he said. "Now you have a chance, boy. Though . . . I will still give you one last chance to simply let me take the bell and live." He picked up his mace, which somehow looked even more threatening without the armor. "Step aside."

"I . . . can't," said Jenks weakly. "The bell binds our Light. Its toll staves off the dark. It is the heart of this town."

In his mind, Jenks saw the faces of his parents, his uncles and aunts, his cousins—each member of the family who had ridden off to war. It was as if, in that moment, they were with him, conjured by his need and the threat of this barbarian. Jenks felt his father's hand on his shoulder; he felt his mother's kiss on his cheek. And if that hand and those lips were cold, then it was no colder than the ice in Jenks's veins.

Help me, he begged in his thoughts. *Akarat, guide my sword hand. Give me speed and wisdom.*

The barbarian filled the space in front of him, as real and as deadly as all the hate and horror in the world.

Jenks shook his head. "I can't let you take that from us. I can't."

"You must," said Klath-Ulna. "There is nothing you can do that will stop me. No, let me say it this way—there is nothing you can do that will matter. Nothing that happens here will be remembered. There will be no ballads, no poems. Nothing. Only dust blown in time's indifferent winds."

Jenks wanted to cry. He wanted to scream. He wanted to run away and hide.

Instead, with what strength he could summon, he raised the sword that had never before seen battle, the blade that had never tasted blood.

"I will not let you," he said. "If you try to take the bell, I, Jenks Grindelson of Saint's Calling, will strike you down. This I swear."

Klath-Ulna sighed.

He actually did not want to kill the lad. Not from pity, for he had little of that, but because it was a pointless fight. This boy was nothing to him. There was no glory in slaughtering a beardless youth in a town full of cowards.

He raised his battle-mace and let Jenks see it. The heavy weapon was covered in runes, each of which was stamped with gold from another bell that he had taken from a tower in another Zakarum town.

"I offered you life, boy," he said. "But you crave death, and that you shall have."

But it was Jenks who struck first.

Jenks knew he had one chance, and that was surprise. He swung the sword in a circle over his head, and as he dropped to the lower step, he brought it down, using all of his weight, the weight of the sword, and all of his fear to power that strike.

Klath-Ulna moved with shocking speed, pulling his naked chest back away from the slashing blade. Even so, the tip of Jenks's sword drew a hot red line from collarbone to ribs. Blood welled, dark red in the shadows of the church.

Jenks did not stand and gape but instead rushed forward, slashing again and again, hoping to end this quickly, knowing that he could not risk letting the barbarian regain his balance.

Klath-Ulna dodged the second blow and used the bottom of his balled fist to smash the third stroke away.

"You're fast, boy." He laughed, clearly impressed. "And you have heart. You can die knowing that you drew blood when many of your betters never could."

And then he raised the battle-mace and swung it at Jenks's head.

The weapon had to weigh a hundred pounds, but Klath-Ulna swung it like it was a willow wand. Jenks screamed and ducked as the massive battle-mace tore through the air inches from his head. The weapon struck the front door of the church and smashed it to kindling. Splinters flew like arrows. Jenks felt a dozen points of pain and then the hot flow of blood.

Klath-Ulna whipped the mace again, this time at waist height. Jenks dropped into a frog crouch, then sprang up, driving the point of his sword forward.

He never saw the punch that struck his chest. All he knew was that he was flying backward through the ruin of the doors. He hit the floor inside and slid a dozen yards. Somehow, the sword was still in his hand, but his entire chest felt like it was crushed. He rolled onto hands and knees, coughing, shocked that he was still alive.

Behind him, the remains of the door blew apart as the battle-mace struck once more. And then Klath-Ulna was inside, stalking toward him as he raised his weapon.

Jenks launched himself forward, tucking into a roll as the battle-mace crashed down onto the floor. The impact once more picked Jenks up and hurled him sideways. He hit a row of pews and knocked them over, one after another as if tiles in a game.

"Akarat save me," cried Jenks as he fought to rise. He saw Klath-Ulna striding down the aisle, and Jenks spun and ran.

The door to the tower was a stout one, heavy oak banded in iron. Jenks slammed it behind him and shot the bolt. There was a bookstand with hymnals inside, and he shoved it against the door.

Then he ran up the winding staircase, pausing at each landing to shove furniture down the stairs. There was a half-cask of lamp oils, and he poured this down the steps to make them slick.

The door below shuddered as it was struck. Once. Twice. And then it crashed inward, the wood shattered and the iron bands twisted. Popped rivets pinged and banged off the walls.

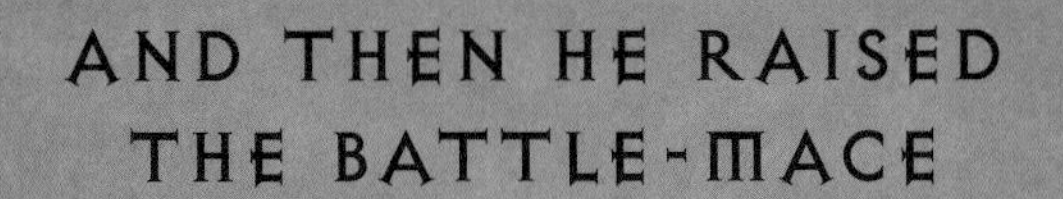

AND SWUNG IT AT
JENKS'S HEAD.

Klath-Ulna pushed through and looked up. For a moment, he and Jenks beheld each other. The killer still wore his smile, but there was something different about it. Was he impressed by this level of resistance? Jenks thought so, though it would offer scant comfort when he was dead.

The barbarian climbed the stairs, smashing the frail defenses without haste. Jenks ran up and up and finally could run no farther. The bell was there. Iron. Pure. Holy.

Jenks placed one hand on it, his mind filling with desperate prayers.

May the Light grant me strength. Akarat, be with me now. I need you. I'm trying my best, but I can't do this alone. Help me!

Outside, clouds parted and a beam of pure, clean sunlight slanted down through the belfry. It painted his face and body with gold and filled his heart with renewed courage. He adjusted his grip on the sword and raised it so that the sunlight—the precious Light—would touch the steel and lend its gift of grace. Jenks felt fresh power in his arms.

He looked at the bell, and through tears he cried, "I swear I will not let him take you. On my life I swear."

Then he heard the footfall behind him.

He turned as Klath-Ulna stepped onto the belfry platform.

"Why are you willing to die to defend this bell?"

"It isn't just the bell," protested Jenks. "This is my church, my faith. I have the Light on my side."

Klath-Ulna lowered his weapon and shook his head. "You have no idea how the world works, do you, boy? You *think* you do, but faith is not the same as understanding. That's what is wrong with this world. Innocents like you willing to die pointless deaths. You think that because you stand in the Light it is your armor. You believe that protecting this bell is what you were born for—*destined* for. You are blind to the truth, Jenks of Saint's Calling. You cannot see past what you have been taught, and that is the chink in your armor. I know this, for I have fought many—*many*—who believed as you believe. The Light did not save them then, and it will not save you now."

"You lie! I know the truth. You are the agent of evil, and I stand with Akarat. This church, this bell—this is holy, and your lies can't change that."

"I like your spirit, boy," said Klath-Ulna. "Truly. I have fought champions and kings with less heart. You remind me of someone—a friend, a brother—with whom I first went to war. He was like you—the courage of ten men. But alas . . . courage isn't enough. Purity of soul is not enough. None of that saved my friend. I wept for him and slew his slayer. And I learned the cruelty of this world and its false beliefs firsthand."

He paused. "I don't want to kill you. I *should*, but I make the same offer. Give me the bell, and I will spare you and this town. Your *heart* can save your friends and family, lad, but I must have the bell. Now . . . step aside."

Jenks was weeping now, and he did not care. He hefted his sword once more.

"I have sworn my life to protect Saint's Calling. This bell *is* the town. If you take it, then what does my life matter? I will always be the one who failed the town and failed my church." He gave a slow, stubborn shake of his head. "You will have to kill me to take it, and I will not make that easy."

Klath-Ulna stared at him. "You even *sound* like my friend."

There was such deep sadness in his eyes that for one shining moment, Jenks thought that the killer would yield, would turn and leave.

However, in his heart, doubt had been sown, and he could feel it take root in the soil of his soul.

"No," Jenks said. "The Light is pure. It is true."

The Light was warm against his cheek; it made everything so clear. He raised the sword above his head and shouted a prayer.

No one appeared to save him.

With a heavy sigh, Klath-Ulna raised his weapon too.

Klath-Ulna went down to the street. For the first time in more years than he could count, the battle-mace felt heavy. Or maybe it was his heart, weighed down by memories of his lost friend. And by what he had just done.

The spikes of his mace glistened with hot crimson. The belfry was painted with splashes of blood. The boy had died hard. He'd fought all the way to the end, even past the point where he knew he was dying. With a shattered chest and one broken arm, with the bones of his cheek grinding together, one eye blind and the other seeing through a red veil, Jenks fought. With a mouth full of broken teeth, he shouted prayers to the Light and curses to Klath-Ulna. Mauled and maimed and dying, he tried to stand fast between the barbarian and the bell.

He died, still holding his sword. Even then, even as he fell and with a broken blade, the boy tried to stab Klath-Ulna.

The last paladin of Saint's Calling was dead. Klath-Ulna stood above him, watching the broken chest rise and fall, rise and fall . . . and rise no more. His frustration for this pointless combat almost made him kick the sword from the boy's hand.

Almost.

Instead, the barbarian stood for a long moment in a kind of vigil. He had not done such a thing since his friend had perished long ago. He saw the shadow of his old companion in the death mask of Jenks Grindelson.

"Damn you, boy," he breathed.

Then he left and took the bell with him.

When he stepped out into the street, his armor once more buckled on, there were a dozen townsfolk in the square, each of them clutching some kind of weapon. They saw the bell and they

IN EVERY SHADOW,
HE COULD SEE THE
BOY'S EYES,

COULD FEEL HIS
WEIGHT OF BELIEF,
OF PURPOSE.

did not see Jenks, and Klath-Ulna watched how that changed their faces. Rage and hurt, fear and defeat.

He walked toward them. When they began to close around him, he merely said, "No."

Just that.

They turned away, weeping, and he walked out of Saint's Calling.

In the mountains a half-day's walk, he stopped where his horse was tethered. He removed a cauldron that was hung from the saddle, built a fire, and as night fell, he used a file to cut eyeholes and a mouth slit into the armor. Then he tried it on. What had been a bell to the townsfolk fitted perfectly as a helmet to him. As it should have. It completed the entire suit of armor he wore, and that was well. He stood for a long time in the moonlight, eyes closed, arms wide, fists clenched.

He removed his full set of armor from the packhorse and put it on. He fitted the helmet and stood ready to feel complete, to feel the roaring pride that had driven him for so long. This was the final act of a journey that had consumed so many years of his life.

But the helmet sat heavy upon him. His pride melted into melancholy as he thought about the boy. Jenks.

Despite being so badly misled by his belief in the Light, the boy had been pure. True. Brave.

Klath-Ulna felt that purity burning on his skin like flame. In every shadow, he could see the boy's eyes, could feel his weight of belief, of purpose.

He turned away toward his horse, and in those few steps, the pieces of armor clanged strangely. It was as if each separate item sought to haunt him with an echo of each bell that he had gathered to forge them. It made him stop and even sent a shiver through his flesh.

He took the reins of his horse, but before he mounted, Klath-Ulna looked back the way he'd come. Back to Saint's Calling.

There were other boys in that town. Other young ones growing in strength and in the purity of their belief. He wondered if the echoes of his clanking armor would be like bells that would call them to war. Had taking the bell given a new sense of purpose and strength to the next generation of paladins? Would they come looking for him, or others like him?

Without doubt.

It saddened him to know that this was not mere thought. It was prophecy.

He closed his eyes for a long moment, and then he mounted the horse, turned its head, and rode off into the east.

I was not there, but I have seen these things. I, Tejal, am cursed with such knowledge, such insights.

There was no true victor of that battle. Anyone who says differently does not understand how history unfolds or how the human heart works.

Klath-Ulna did not win that fight. The boy, Jenks, did not lose it.

Jenks became a legend among his own people. Because of how he made his stand, even though he died, so many other young people in Saint's Calling put down their cards and dice and picked up swords. Jenks taught them that so much is worth fighting for. Even dying for.

Those swords rise even now, mirror-bright in the fires of war, the sword arms given strength by hope.

As for Klath-Ulna . . . his tale goes on and on. Rivers of gold—and of blood—wait for him. Even after so long a quest to construct a suit of armor from the bells of the churches of a faith that had turned its back on him. With the helmet completing that armor, he believed that he would once more feel whole. That he would be, in some way that even he could not articulate, home.

But there is no home for such as he. There can never be. War calls his name. Blood sings to his soul. Conquest demands his loyalty. He will spill and shed much, but after Saint's Calling . . . those who know him whisper that he was never thereafter the same.

Instincts

A SHORT STORY BY

RYAN QUINN

INSTINCTS

Twilight in eastern Kingsport was when everyone around started to vanish. Alodie was used to it, the sudden way the city got inhospitable, but she was no less bothered for the familiarity.

She walked with purpose as she traversed the street, more an outdoor tunnel, really, the cramped path sloping endlessly down in the dark. On either side were sodden old wood homes, divided and divided again until it was impossible to chop them any smaller. Then they were just lean-tos, hovels for the wretched and the poor.

Mewls Avenue's dwellings hid it well from everywhere else. At least Alodie could smell the ocean here, though she couldn't see it. Shouts and curses carried from the docks. Most corners were dead ends. Sad fish gagged their last somewhere out of sight. It stunk.

One saving grace for Kingsport's slums: nobody much cared what you were doing. She followed her cousin along mold-flecked cobbles, keeping a body's distance.

"Hurry up," Boyce muttered, walking faster, not looking back at her, *still* not saying where they were headed.

Boyce was older and gaunt, deeper in the blood, with a nose so proud it served as his face from most angles. His coat was big enough to hide a broadsword. Alodie had fair and fine hair bound up tight. She'd put her ugly gloves on. They were dressed to settle someone.

Out of all the things she did for the family in Kingsport, she liked settling people the least.

Organizing was tense work. Preparing the coachmen for a delivery, making sure they knew which crates to open and which ones to keep sealed, and how much to bribe the watch if they got caught . . . Alodie was good with details, but too many left her exhausted at the end of a day. Even so, her allowance was decent. And while shipping manifests were mindless, Alodie could skip out if she finished fast enough. She cut through the dullness by making her nights more memorable. Earlier in the year, she and Linn had gotten dead drunk and wrote "ALMS" in cow's blood on the leather hood of one of the family's carriages.

The carriage looked pristine the next morning. Nobody was punished; nobody even mentioned it. Alodie amused herself for hours just imagining Boyce's old mother, the matriarch herself, her face winding up like a screw, directing the washing woman to take care of it through a string of curses.

Linn had been Alodie's only friend for far too long. Alodie couldn't say exactly what brought them together, though she knew what kept them close: Linn had a poet's spirit. She toiled away in her shop at all hours, but she made sure both of them always had the finest silks to wear out. Alodie envied her. At least Linn wasn't part of the family. She didn't have to settle anyone.

You only settled the worst kind of people. Leeches. First they got in debt, *then* they borrowed, and *then* they tried not to pay.

And Alodie always had to play dealmaker with a leech. Her cousins could get . . . excessive, and she needed to set the dates and the amounts and assuage the leech's fears while the boys stomped around and made a mess. Help the leeches help themselves before they got hurt. Even if most of them deserved to get hurt.

The whole practice—the need for it—was shameful. Why weren't people just better?

Boyce led the way down Nogarden. They were turning angles every few seconds as a maze of wood and stone choked the path around them. If anyone was looking, Alodie couldn't see them for the grime coating the windows. It made sense, people leaving them filthy. Despicable things happened on the other side.

Alodie was lost and a little nauseated. She tried Boyce. "Who's the leech?"

Boyce didn't look back or even acknowledge her question, as usual. He disappeared around a corner.

Rounding it, she saw her cousin fussing with whatever was under his coat. Boyce had finally, blessedly, come to a stop in front of the door to a squat brown row house, one she—

Alodie forgot the thousand annoyances that had strangled her attention all evening. Her heart and her guts dropped through the cobbles. Panic clawed her fingers inward.

The sign for Linn's shop creaked back and forth in the evening breeze.

Boyce smiled at her. His teeth were dingy.

"Toughen up, little sprite," he said. "Indulge the instincts. This'll go quick."

Then he turned and kicked the door open.

"*How* could you be so stupid?" Alodie screamed at her only friend.

Alodie was glad she couldn't see herself. She knew what she must look like. Spit flying, veins protruding in her neck and forehead, face flushed to full claret. A real grotesque.

They'd tied Linn to a chair in her shop, bound her hands together behind it, then tipped it over, pressing her against the ground. Just to keep her scared. The place was already a muddle. Heaps of wool and rabbit fur surrounded a loom on the back wall. Leather hanging in uneven strands; jars of clumpy dyes on the lone desk; straw everywhere on the floor. The ceiling was low and saggy enough to dump the upstairs tenants on top of them.

Opposite the clutter, in an open dresser, sat yards of fine silk, neatly folded.

Alodie pointed at the silk. One of the family's deliveries. She swept her finger around the room. "We gave you all of this. The only thing you needed to do was pay on time."

Linn couldn't stop her tears. Her tiny face was apple-shaped, and the crying made it seem smaller. An intricate blue-and-gold ascot wound around her neck; she'd pampered her short auburn hair with rose powder and wax she'd stolen from the tanner. Alodie knew that for certain; she'd been the lookout.

The expression Linn wore was fully pleading. *Good.* It meant she'd be amenable. Alodie put a hand on the chair, as if to stand her up. "If you can just get us two hundred back in a month—"

Boyce interrupted. "Can't keep a promise, don't make one." He was a boor, and he sounded like it.

Immediately, Linn's face went defiant. As defiant as she could be with all seven stone of her crushed into the ground.

"Sard yourself, pinch-nose," she spat. "I hope your mum's cats eat her eyes and demons eat the cats."

Linn was never a boor. She had a point too: Boyce's mother was awful.

Boyce didn't say anything, just opened his coat and brought out a twin head hammer. He put it through the dye jars one at a time, sprinkling glass and cobalt-colored pulp throughout the shop. Linn screamed. Alodie covered her eyes when the glass flew, checked for cuts when it stopped, didn't feel any.

Then Boyce was stuffing a rag in Linn's mouth, flipping the chair back over, and heading to the desk with his hammer.

"Stop," Alodie shouted, loud, before he could do something else ugly.

"And what do I get if I stop?" Boyce said, waving the hammer. He looked back and forth between the two of them, like he was their problem to solve.

Alodie glanced at Linn's face: mouth open, eyes big, brows stretched up. Terrified.

"She won't just pay it back. She'll give you an extra hundred gold, on the side, when it's done. For your trouble. In a month. Right, Linn?"

Linn nodded. In settling, this was progress. One show of force, and—

Boyce took a long, deliberate step toward Alodie. He had a tight grip on the hammer.

"I don't think she'd learn from that. I think"—he drew out the wait—"that's *undeserved* leniency."

Alodie's heart was pounding. Hopefully nobody could see it on her face. Now she had to settle both of them.

"All right," she said. "Linn pays in two weeks. I'll come pick it up. And I'll take care of your manifests for a month." A concession. Sometimes, concessions could be good. They showed you respected the other party.

"You really don't have the instincts," Boyce said, flexing his fingers around the hammer. He almost sounded sad.

His mother spoke fondly about the instincts, so Boyce did too. They used it to keep her down, when they knew full well she could run the whole operation. So they said she lacked a hunter's instincts. A killer's.

But Alodie had them. She'd proven it.

Up to a point.

"I think, if she's going to take our livelihood, we should take hers. That makes sense." Boyce turned, raised his hammer, and looked down at Linn, scrunched under the chair.

Linn shrank back, moaned something around the gag.

"Please," Alodie said.

Boyce held on to the chair to steady it.

Alodie knew what he was thinking. The instincts took over.

"You're an imbecile. If you break her knuckles, how exactly do you expect her to come up with the coin? She'll—"

He brought the hammer down, hard.

Linn thrashed around under the chair. Everything she tried to say was wordless inchoate nonsense. Not just because of the gag. Because she couldn't help herself. Because it hurt too much.

She was shivering and drooling as Boyce pulled the chair up and unfastened her wrists. Linn's right knuckles were crushed to pits, blood flowing up everywhere—under the nails, in the ragged little rents splitting her skin. She rocked back and forth, cradling one arm in the other.

Alodie didn't want to see. She made herself stare at Boyce—who, beyond a little sweat, didn't look like he'd done much of anything at all.

"Now we're getting nothing," Alodie sneered at him, hateful as she felt. "Less than nothing, you idiot."

Boyce just shrugged. "She'll pay. Got a faster way to make it back than a couple weeks' work." With one hand, he pulled Linn toward the door. She was still wailing behind the gag.

His nonchalance made Alodie cold. "Where are you taking her?"

What was he thinking? Selling her to a prize house? Selling her into labor? With her hand ruined like that?

Boyce ignored Alodie again. "She's not your problem anymore."

Then he kicked a rucksack at her feet. Straw swirled in the air. "Get the silk, take anything else worthwhile, and go home. We'll talk tomorrow."

Alodie's face burned red. She should stop him. Hit him. Do something.

But he was deeper in the blood.

Linn didn't take her eyes off Alodie as Boyce dragged her from the shop.

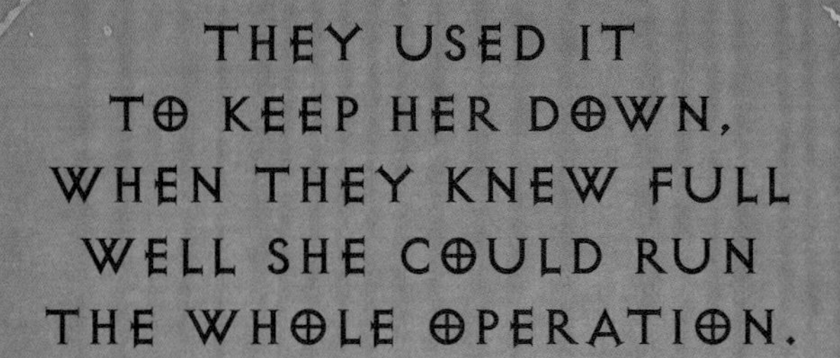

THEY USED IT
TO KEEP HER DOWN,
WHEN THEY KNEW FULL
WELL SHE COULD RUN
THE WHOLE OPERATION.

SO THEY SAID SHE LACKED
A HUNTER'S INSTINCTS.
A KILLER'S.

Alodie went through the slums like she was ripping out a stitch. Slow. Backward. Feeling more than she'd wanted.

She'd never bothered to help a leech when settling didn't work. But Linn wasn't a leech. Or at least, not an *ordinary* leech.

You didn't praise a leech's talent to your family. You didn't invite her to the table to deal.

When a leech did well for herself, the two of you didn't storm the upper district, dressed better than the gentry. Wantons and troubadours didn't fawn over you. Your nights didn't go so deliciously late the sun was scared to show its face.

You didn't promise a leech you would watch out for her. And she didn't promise you the same.

Maybe Linn thought she would get special treatment from the family because they were close. Maybe Alodie had let her think that.

So she stayed farther behind Boyce this time, out of sight, leaning against the chophouses scattered around Mewls until the slums went straight again. Alodie walked a scattered way; a drifter, not a hunter. When Boyce met up with a few more night-shapes and they shoved something dark and bundled onto a cart, Alodie picked up her pace just barely. A drifter with purpose.

Her cousin's cart rolled over the filthy cobbles, west and north. Four figures and a cart: a prelude to a shipment. Their evening would be bigger than Linn.

But they were headed away from the docks. At least they weren't shipping her to Bilefen.

Alodie followed Boyce's crew for an hour without stopping, out of the always-yawning north gates with their flamboyant blue-green banners, and onto the trail roads. She crept in the dark, with no more slums to hide her, starting at every owl sound. The little dots of their torches led her off the trail and toward the woods, where the smell of the sea fled for rich, rotting earth.

Then she waited. Gave them a few minutes to get ahead before she started moving. Alodie had a fairly good idea of where they were going.

The family kept a coach stop miles out of town, in the thinnest part of the Solterwood, for swapping riders and cargo before starting on new trips. Alodie had made the walk there more than once.

The stop was well hidden, right where the tree canopy started to get thick. Boyce dusted his hands behind a big four-wheeled carriage; two other carriages sat yards beyond. All three were hooded in plain leather, open-backed but dim inside, their cargo concealed.

Alodie could hear their horses huffing and stamping, and muffled chatter between the coachmen. She crouched low to the forest floor, hands down in the worms and moss and scat. Shrubs and brambles pried at her skin.

Boyce and his crew, squash-head Lachlan and two other thick-necks, turned and shuffled toward her in the dark, toting weighty

MAYBE A GOOD BIT
OF THE INSTINCTS

WAS JUST IGNORING
CONSEQUENCES.

clubs and torches that doubled as clubs. Some of the family's people had come over from the knife gangs, she remembered.

They were grim-faced and dead quiet to a one. Usually, a handoff brought out some ill humor. Talk about how they'd spend the money, if nothing else. And they walked faster than they had on the way up, their heads swiveling about like gophers. As if they wanted to put the place behind them.

Alodie bit her tongue hard. She felt the throb of new pain as they brought their torches closer and closer. To illuminate the night. To find her hiding in a bush.

She looked at Boyce. Really looked at him. He was deeper in the blood, but he wasn't invincible. His eyes were mostly black pupils, soft and supple jelly all. His throat narrow and bare enough to crush. If only she'd thought to bring a sap, a sharp stick, even a gloveful of broken glass from the shop floor.

He walked right at her. Alodie tensed her fists, bent at the knees. If they found her, she'd wish she'd struck first.

And then what? Get her knuckles crushed. Get sold into labor. Boyce had been absolutely right: She didn't have the instincts. She was pretending.

Or she wasn't listening hard enough. He *was* distracted. Letting him ignore her, letting him get away with it—that was an opportunity. The instincts knew.

Soundlessly, Alodie sunk closer to the undergrowth.

The crew marched past Alodie's hideaway, swift and

determined. Their torchlight receded from view. She found herself swaddled in enough shadow to breathe. Ahead, three carriages creaked, kicking up soil and dirt in their wake, lead horses tugging them forward at the crack of a whip.

Step out too fast, and the family would see. But if the horses got up to speed, she would never catch them.

Keeping her eyes off Boyce's crew, imagining them still withdrawing with their backs turned, Alodie crept to the closest carriage. She held her breath tight, begging herself not to cough as equine stink and forest rot washed over her.

At the front of each carriage sat a coachman, with a long horsewhip and a pair of mounted torches flanking their seat. They fussed with their whips, calling out commands to each other. Whistling. Shouting. Occupied. The lead horses started to gallop.

Maybe a good bit of the instincts was just ignoring consequences.

Alodie lunged. She got one foot on the step at the back of the carriage car and heaved herself up and in. She landed hard on her belly, felt the wind fly out of her.

Grateful for being breathless, given the hell she found.

The inside of the carriage was a portrait of misery. Bodies slumped atop one another, crushed up against the walls. Ragged gray forms taking wheezing half-breaths, trussed to iron posts like coneys. A few were unshod, with their feet broken and purple at the knobs, or their hands smashed into ruins of dangling nails. Most had been blindfolded; all were gagged. Heads lolled in stupor. Lit by tiny threads of torchlight from above, they were more like silhouettes than people.

Boyce's mother—the whole family, Alodie included—shipped a lot of things. Things they shouldn't have. But this was beyond what she knew.

Alodie sucked in a breath she didn't want.

She couldn't stand, and not just for the sick upheaval in her stomach. The carriage moved fast. Rolling forward, the horses pulling them straight north, where the trees were denser. That route would make the Solterwood impassible on the wheel after too long. Where in the Hells were they going?

Alodie looked frantically across the faces of the condemned, avoiding the unfocused eyes of the ones who looked back. She didn't recognize a single one. Probably they'd been leeches. Surely they weren't any of *her* leeches.

She felt frantic then, as if she would start weeping, but the instincts wouldn't let her. Everything poured into the clod in her throat.

Linn lay in the back, nearly atop two other prisoners. Eyes closed, bound and gagged. Still.

Alodie pushed herself up to a crouch. "Shh," she whispered to the passengers, putting a finger to her lips. Not really talking. Hearing her own voice talk. Tapping herself for emphasis.

"Need to get her. Then I'll help." Could she help these wretches? Did it matter?

A dull moan rejoined. From near the wall, a shuddering, pitiful inhale. Alodie wasn't sure they heard. Or understood.

She tried for all the authority she could fit into a whisper. "Don't make a sound."

Alodie inched forward, feeling every movement of her hands, trying not to touch their agonized limbs. Close to the front of the carriage, she saw Linn's eyes flutter, and the wash of relief staggered her.

Linn's eyes were puffy. But she looked back, and Alodie saw recognition in them. She hadn't been drugged, Alodie figured—the good fortune of being a late addition to the shipment. But the rag in her mouth had been swapped for a leather gag, and both her hands were bound tightly to a post.

Her right hand was a travesty, ugly purple-yellow and swollen. Broken, surely. Beyond a healer, likely. There were a lot of bits to make a hand work.

Leaves and branches scraped along the sides of the carriage. The forest was getting denser. Alodie gingerly tried to remove the rope on Linn's wrists. Then she'd free her feet, then get the gag. Then they would run.

As she fought with Linn's bindings, Alodie's hands trembled. For all that she could control them, they might as well have been someone else's. At least the ugly gloves soaked up her sweat. But there were so many knots. No fray points. It was taking too long.

In frustration, she tried to work one of the loops over Linn's good wrist. Linn whimpered into the gag and clenched her eyes shut, taking panicked snorts of air, each minute mounting agony.

Then Alodie heard the coachmen shouting, and the carriage started to slow. She pulled frantically at Linn's bonds.

Meager torchlight vanished above them. Someone dropped from the coach seat onto the forest floor, squelching in the soil. Alodie swiveled to the back of the carriage, but the footfalls moved quickly around the front, followed by the sounds of horses getting unhooked. They clomped noisily away. The coachmen were running.

No one entered the carriage. Had they been abandoned?

Linn tried to say something around the gag. Knowing her, it would be a joke about her mangled hand. *Looks a beauty, don't it?* Or maybe she would be furious. She had every right.

Alodie got Linn's good wrist free and yanked the gag loose.

"They ain't shipping us out," Linn whispered, ragged. "We're bait."

From outside, Alodie heard the sound of timber splintering in multiple places at once, a tumult of axe blows falling on the forest entire.

One horrified scream ripped through the air. A chorus followed.

A minute passed in the shape of an hour. The shrieking outside the carriage began to shift. Wet, low gurgling took its place. Alodie could hear frenzied scrabbling, a different, throat-shredding yell, then silence.

The instincts quailed in her. Every impulse melted into fear. Her breaths burned. She could barely move. She mostly just trembled.

With one working hand, Linn worried at the bonds on her own feet, saying nothing. Her progress was hobbled, slower than the death that stalked them. She'd never get loose alone.

The condemned were coming to life now, glancing around sluggishly, trying to drag themselves off their posts, wringing at ropes and sweat-slick leather straps.

Alodie had to be the only person in the carriage halfway to her feet. Free to run. Linn looked up at her, wondering. Asking. She had every right.

Linn only nodded when Alodie leaned down and got a thumb under the bonds on her feet. They worked at it together, until the slow scrape of something heavy dragging along the soil assailed Alodie's ears. It was all she could think about while she tugged the rope over Linn's left foot, shredding skin.

Until the front of the carriage split in half.

Wood splinters exploded around them. Alodie scrabbled backward, tugging Linn by her good arm.

The carriage tilted. Three of the condemned vanished, ripped

THE SHRIEKING
OUTSIDE THE CARRIAGE
BEGAN TO SHIFT. WET, LOW
GURGLING TOOK ITS PLACE.
ALODIE COULD HEAR

FRENZIED SCRABBLING,
A DIFFERENT, THROAT-
SHREDDING YELL,
THEN SILENCE.

bodily off their posts and into the dark. Screams burst forth from everywhere at once.

Alodie caught a glimpse of ink-stained gums and rows upon rows of teeth. A serrated red-black tendril flicked through the ruin, catching her across the shoulder. She tore herself away from it painfully, and it snaked away to drag another of the condemned out of view. Alodie didn't look at the other prisoners, just heaved Linn forward. They scurried out over the carriage's bent back.

Linn took a child's steps, limping on legs numb from her bindings. Alodie's shoulder buzzed with pain as they lurched forward, in the deep of a wood neither recognized. Behind her, Alodie could see the wreck of all three carriages, red-splattered, blood coating them thick as yolk. A chamber torch, stubbornly ensconced and still burning, jutted atop one like a candle.

The bodies of the family's offering were everywhere behind. Red, ropy innards trailed from them, bunched and pulled like marionette strings. All of them, dead and half-dead and not-dead, writhed in unison on the ground, matching one another's movements, one another's noises.

Heart pounding, Alodie pulled Linn along the loam, deeper into the Solterwood's shadows, as fast as the instincts would allow her.

INSTINCTS

An abomination stalked the Solterwood with blood on its claws. Slunk low to the ground, it moved like a whisper.

Trees crowded out the moonlight but could not dissuade it. Its eyes were made for the darkness.

As it had many times before, the abomination lingered on hours-old ruin: two grievously wounded corpses, the remnants of their flesh hewn by claw and fang. What little skin remained to them was spiny, different than it had once been.

The bodies lay on ochre-stained soil. Both were still. That was important.

The abomination prodded at the bodies, then punched a hand through one. It bore down with a squelch, *the corpse wooden and unmoving.*

Then it loomed over the second one. Repeated.

This corpse opened its dislocated jaws wide, hissing rotten mucus from between its teeth. Like a dying insect, it flailed at the abomination with every limb. Even in this state, its strikes were brutal. The razorlike prongs poking up through its skin scraped against the abomination's hide but could not find purchase.

The abomination twisted. With a crunch, *the corpse fell still. Its eyes were sunken, encrusted all around with red rheum. In all its frenzy, the lids had never once opened.*

Rising to its feet, seeking past the sweet smoke and putrefaction, the abomination found something else. Its gaze fell on scattered tracks, trailing east to the densest part of the wood. It pawed at the dirt, stopped, inhaled.

Two more. Both blooded.

The hunt would not end here.

Shadows coiled around the abomination, and it was gone.

Alodie and Linn fled from the things in the night. The darkness was impenetrable. More of the forest seemed to just emerge around them with every step.

Alodie was steering Linn with both hands. And the instincts were steering her. No one was in control.

They had run for what felt like hours, harried by brush cracking and wet, ferine snarls. The hair on Alodie's neck stood up without ceasing. It was like she was being watched, always, but she couldn't see how. Or by whom.

Every few minutes, they'd been forced to stop. Linn would slow and need to rest. Or she'd fall before Alodie could catch her. This time, the wound on her hand had bled through the cloth they'd wrapped around it.

"Do you think it's gone? That . . . thing?" Linn asked. She was slumped in the grass, trying to keep her breath quiet.

"We should move like it isn't," Alodie said.

Linn just winced and pulled at her makeshift bandage, rearranging it like that would fix something.

"It's not so bad. Boyce has done much worse," Alodie said, helping her up.

"*Now* you feel like helping?" Linn sneered as she rose from the bramble.

"I'm here, aren't I?" Alodie said, trying her best to keep them moving. "I would have told you if I'd known."

Linn was quiet.

Concessions could be good. She tried again. "If I had done anything, they would probably have killed us both."

Linn stared at her, dumbfounded. Maybe mad at herself for not realizing what a nightmare she'd cozied up to. Maybe madder at Alodie for letting her.

"You know, normally the smart ones pay on time." Alodie tried to keep the criticism out of her voice. It didn't work.

Linn shoved away from her and walked on her own. It was even slower going.

"And you've never been in a rut, have you, Miss Alodie?" Linn spat back. "Nobody wanted to come down to Mewls for months. I tried taking orders in the Upper. Things just slowed."

Despite herself, Alodie felt the instincts surging, spoiling for a fight she could win. "So you decided to have us carry the debt for you?"

"'Us'?" Linn was incredulous. "You know how much money they have. You're always talking about how shite they all are—why do you care if I need a couple weeks?"

"I don't," Alodie said, realizing. She let the fight lapse. Linn deserved to have this, at least.

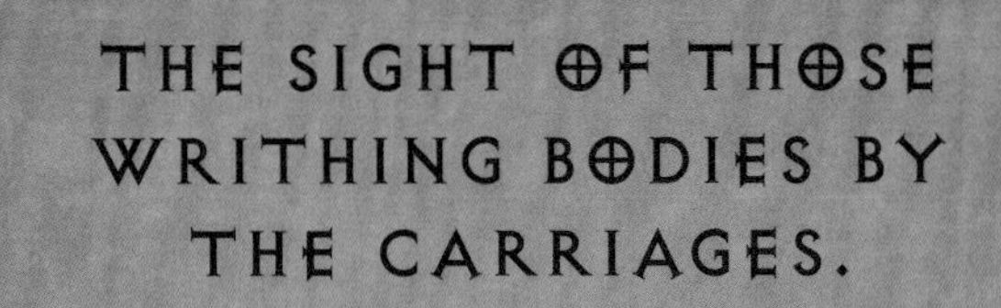

THE SIGHT OF THOSE
WRITHING BODIES BY
THE CARRIAGES.

THEY WAY THEY MOVED
LIKE PUPPETS . . . THAT,
SHE COULDN'T FORGET.

Alodie reached out to help her over some misshapen roots. "When they're coming by for your other hand, I'll give you a warning first."

Linn just stared back, face all ashen misery. "You don't get to joke about it."

Alodie had gone too far. It hadn't even been a night.

"Not until I joke about it a couple times." Linn smirked. "Ideally with an audience."

The forest was quieter. Tentatively, they settled into a slow walk. A shared pace.

In an hour, they'd heard no sounds of pursuit and seen nothing else alive. The forest seemed stripped of its chatter, and there was no sign of the night giving way or of the forest thinning out. They were both shivering.

From far off, Alodie heard a noise she recognized. A dying horse, whinnying around a mouthful of fluid. As they drew closer, she saw its belly had been opened. Linn looked away and covered her face with her good arm.

Alodie stopped to help her lean against an oak and searched near where the horse had fallen. She returned with a torch and a strikebox, then took Linn by the shoulder. "Are you going to . . . ?" Linn asked, leaving the question unfinished.

Alodie ignored her. Hustled them both away, fast.

She'd watched coachmen put down horses before. It was always sad, seeing the trust in their eyes. But at least she could tuck that away. The sight of those writhing bodies by the carriages, the way they moved like puppets . . . that, she couldn't forget.

If an animal was dying here, still making noise, that could be a distraction. Whatever was hunting them could go hunt something else.

She veered opposite their path, driving Linn on, moving south. What she hoped was south—the trees were too thick to see the stars. The grainy, wet soil started to give way to rocks, shards of granite that scraped her boots. Linn tripped even more often, breathed heavier, walked with her head down. Alodie stumbled a few times herself. They made a sluggard's pace in the dark, but the Solterwood thinned, ever so slightly, until they nearly smacked into a wall.

They were leaning against cold, mossy granite. A cave mouth yawned open a few dozen feet from them. Shelter.

Relief flooded Alodie. The constant feeling of being watched receded.

Alodie laid the torch on dry rocks, hunched over it with the strikebox open. She began pounding flint and steel, then blowing on an ugly gloveful of tinder. It was awkward and imperfect work, but not her first time. The torch burst into flame.

"Now you're not being serious," Lynn said. But she shivered. Her voice was questioning, not demanding. She wanted to be wrong.

"Are you thinking we just walk until we collapse? We'll be safer if nothing can sneak up on us," Alodie reasoned. She motioned Linn forward.

They paced into the cave, the torch high above Alodie's head, feeling their way along the cave walls. An open area, somewhere to wait out the night, was all they needed. They hurried, drawing on the vigor of a second chance.

The torch was their lodestar. As they walked, Alodie felt it scrape the cave's ceiling. She wanted to hold it high, to send its light far ahead.

"How long do we need to be at this?" Linn asked, huffing. Where her fear had receded, her pain was filling the gaps.

Alodie's throat was so dry she cleared it twice before she could answer. "We should go deep enough that it would take work to get us out. Somewhere wide open, where we can keep our eye on the entrance." Alodie wasn't sure. She just wanted to sound sure. "Then I can take watch for a few hours, keep the torch lit. So you can get some rest."

They left the moonlit parts of the tunnel behind. The cave's walls were humid and wet, the stone occasionally hiding tiny beads of moisture that made her hands slip. Alodie certainly wasn't looking forward to sleeping on the ground. But they had to make it through. Linn had to make it through.

Something scraped at the cave wall behind them.

"Shhh." Alodie turned the torch, scanning the area as best she could. She didn't see anything near in the dimness. But the sound was back the way they'd come.

They backed up, scrambling deeper into the cave, down the corridor. Ahead, it split in two.

Alodie drove them left, ensuring Linn was in front of her, nearly shoving her to keep them moving.

Another maze in the dark. Alodie brought them to a turn, took it right—and realized they'd walked an elbow. The cave doubled back on itself.

A sound like an axe-head hitting stone reverberated through the cavern.

Her whole body was paralyzed with fear. Alodie stood unmoving, just pointed Linn down the right corridor. That was all she could manage. Linn looked back at her. Looked ahead again. And started to take shuffling steps forward. Trusted that she wasn't another dying horse.

It couldn't corner both of them. Alodie took the other corridor.

She held the torch as high as she could, gripping it with both hands, careful to avoid the wet walls. She didn't want to see the thing that had ripped the carriage apart. But she had to for them to have any hope of surviving.

Alodie could hear Linn's breathing for a few seconds, and then she outpaced the sound. There were no more scrapes, no more clangs. She would find the thing or Linn would. Alodie followed the torch down this new path. Walked until she noticed the droplets beading on the wall had changed, and stopped for just a second to look at them.

They glistened, reflecting something redder than her torchlight.

Alodie turned from the wall, and a fiend looked back at her. Tendrils jutted from its torso like umbilical cords. Its black-gummed mouth bristled with canines and too many tongues, each covered in sharklike teeth.

Its eyes were pits, merciless but not mindless. Too keen. Too human. Fine brocades that would have been genteel a century ago clung to its waist in tatters. She'd seen clothes like it in Boyce's mother's home. Handed down from their parents' grandparents.

The horror of her family's arrangement hit her. Alodie knew their business made victims. But she couldn't imagine any human justification for selling people to this thing. Money? Protection against its hunger? A bloodline obligation?

Frantic, Alodie stabbed the torch toward it. Fire was the Light's weapon. She swung it wide, twice, then launched herself forward, pressing the torch against the monstrosity, trying to keep as much distance as she could.

It didn't shriek or recoil as the flames sizzled against its face, just leered at her. Then it swatted the torch away and tore her throat out with its teeth.

Alodie hit the ground slowly, like a stone sinking to the bottom of a pond. She gasped, unable to make the air go where it should.

In the guttering light of her discarded torch, Alodie watched as Linn limped around the other side of the corridor.

The creature turned, cast two of its tendrils out like whips, and Linn fell, screaming.

The tendrils pulled her close. It settled down to feed.

Alodie's head lay in a gummy red pool. Everything was numb. She tried to turn away, but she couldn't.

Darkness took too long to claim her.

At last, the prey took its time to feed. Distracted.

The abomination had watched the two survivors of the carriage move noisily through the forest. At the cavern's mouth, the taller of them cast torchlight all around, signaling.

The abomination had also watched its prey. An old vampire, wrapped in the vestiges of its human wealth. Clever, sharing its hunt with people in Kingsport—staying out of sight, trading for chattel, and spreading its plague faster for it.

The vampire was led by its impulses. It did not know restraint. Did not accept being denied. It would seek the survivors.

It was agile. The abomination had not wanted to fight it on open ground.

But the two survivors had entered a cave. Allowed themselves to be cornered. Offered an opportunity.

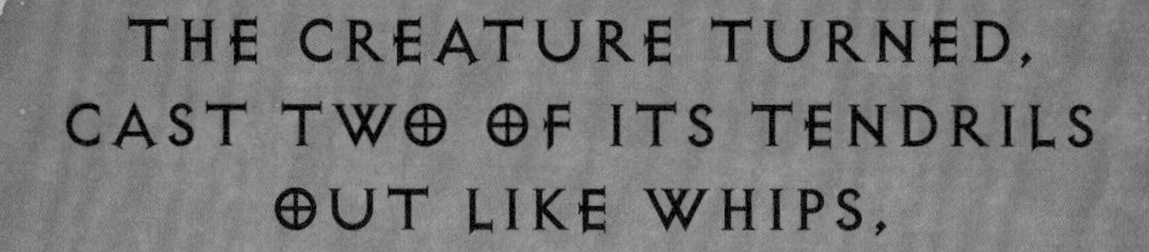

THE CREATURE TURNED,
CAST TWO OF ITS TENDRILS
OUT LIKE WHIPS,

AND LINN FELL, SCREAMING.
THE TENDRILS PULLED
HER CLOSE. IT SETTLED
DOWN TO FEED.

The smell of blood wafted out of the cave mouth.

It brought Zebediah back to himself.

He was tall, with a beaked nose and long, cloud-white hair he left loose. He had a broad, square face, plain and pale but for the most obvious sign of the curse—sunken red eyes, surrounded by spiderwebbing black veins.

Zebediah wore polished armor, ornamental enough for an old Kehjan court, with brilliant crimson plates horizontal along the abdomen. An ampoule on a chain was fitted tight to the gorget of his armor, the vial filled with green-blue water from the river where he had nearly breathed his last, cornered by beasts he'd thought to draw off alone. To spare others—that had been the highest good he knew, back when he was more like a child.

His weighty gear was unusual for a hunt in the Solterwood. For anyone hoping to move quickly and quietly through the forest. Yet he had been called to the service of the Annulet as one of their blood knights for decades. He found it hard to change his ways; they had become indistinguishable from his pledge. *All that remains of my life, weighed against the darkness.*

Every time his journey became impossible, he found his way back to the pledge. Few could say it and mean it; in agony, in dilemma, he had lived it. Zebediah had slain comrades grown accursed and cut the rot from the innocent before it could fester. The life after his life was only ever monstrous; to face it and remain himself demanded a soul like ice. Unbending.

Zebediah whispered dead syllables to the night air. Shadows rolled around him like fog, silencing the sounds his boots would make on stone.

The screams from within the cavern had quieted, but Zebediah could still hear the raspy croaking of the vampire as it fed. He walked quickly through the cavern, needing no light to find his way.

The tunnel tightened, the rasping louder and louder to his ears. Near a bend in the passage, he at last saw the vampire hunched low, its tendrils cradling one of its victims, attached to her body like a dozen lampreys.

Zebediah had not expected any of the carriage victims to survive, even these last two. But if their deaths could give him a slight advantage against the vampire, he had been right to wait and watch. Nothing was more important than ending its threat.

Zebediah could cloak his approach, but not his scent. The vampire turned to look at him and sprang to its feet, hissing around a mouthful of jagged tongues.

A purple-black lance of solid shadow materialized in Zebediah's hand, and he hurled it with all his might. Before the vampire could spring away, the lance slammed solidly home, piercing its throat. Its tendrils shot up, struggling to tear away the shadow that ate at its cold flesh.

Somewhere within Zebediah, the curse exulted at the sight of the prey wounded. He forced it down.

Zebediah advanced on the vampire ponderously, knees bent, longspear held in gloved hands. He did not want to smell the rotten blood pouring from its wounds; he had to kill it quickly, before it could heal. He stabbed out, punched two quick holes in its chest, and tensed his whole body for a double-handed swipe—

Four serrated tendrils wrapped around Zebediah's throat and arms, shredding flesh. The pain was more shattering than anything he had experienced—the hundred tiny teeth of the vampire opened sucking wounds that burned, spreading like fire. As the vampire's tendrils constricted, Zebediah's spear fell from his hands. He could feel himself being torn apart.

The tendrils met in the middle of his body. Zebediah melted in a pool of blood.

The vampire paused, hissing, flailing its arms about. It padded forward, tendrils prodding fingerlike at the air. Then it turned back toward the bodies of its victims, insatiable.

A crimson puddle bubbled up behind it, an amorphous body-like mass. The longspear rose with it, clutched in Zebediah's hand, reforming one finger at a time. His human form returned as blood slid off the mass, and he sprang at the vampire's back.

Zebediah tried not to look as he stabbed the creature over and over. But he couldn't help himself. Three holes. Four. Five. There was something enrapturing about their symmetry, about the perfect bursts of black-red ichor that washed over him. He struck with relish, mortifying his enemy, taking strikes he hardly cared to acknowledge.

Until a tendril scraped at the keepsake around Zebediah's neck and tore the chain free from the gorget. This vampire had been hunted by a blood knight before. It *knew.*

Zebediah dropped to the ground, catching his precious keepsake seconds before it could crash upon the stone. The vampire's limbs enveloped him, but the curse was what truly held him. Zebediah's skin stretched and changed; he gave in, growing into a flayed mass of muscle and blood to rival the vampire in strength and hunger both.

The abomination rent the prey in half, tearing off tendrils and a putrefying arm. Tore at it with the claret claws of blood its hands had become.

The prey was slick with gore. Wriggled this way and that. Trying to escape. Escape was impossible.

The abomination swung in a fury, over and over, with no thought of surcease.

Zebediah shook his head like a dog. His hands throbbed in agony. Of all the great distractions that kept him from losing himself, pain had brought him the most clarity. He was pulping the cave wall, had hit it so much he'd cratered the stone a foot deep.

Half the vampire's sloughed-off flesh lay below him. The other half was gone.

Bloody tracks led out of the cave. It had fled.

THE FAIR-HAIRED WOMAN. SHE HAD SEEMED . . . PROUD. HAUGHTY, EVEN.

AND YET HE HAD SEEN HER STRUGGLE WITH HER INSTINCTS. KNOWING HER CRUELTY, USING AND TURNING FROM IT IN EQUAL MEASURE.

He hissed, turned to slam the wall again. The vampire was faster than him; it *knew* about him. He could still try to catch it. If he started now, maybe—

One of the bodies of the women on the ground twitched. Then, a few seconds later, the other. Again.

In unison.

Who had they been before? Siblings, perhaps? Paramours, the casual and affectless way they spoke?

He had come here to slay the vampire. To stop its curse from spreading.

And yet it had spread anyway, because of *his* choices. *His* lack of restraint. *His* curse, from long before he took up the spear.

What was the highest good? The best amends?

The smaller brown-haired woman was a thrill-seeker, with a sense of joy that would have served her well. She had believed she was worth something, even if the world was not.

The fair-haired woman. She had seemed . . . proud. Haughty, even. And yet he had seen her struggle with her instincts. Knowing her cruelty, using and turning from it in equal measure.

A start. He placed the spear and the keepsake on the ground and knelt before them.

Alodie shivered. Shivered with her whole body. It yearned to move, to tear free from her thoughts and her mind, each limb crawling away of its own accord. Her sight was buried, a pinprick of seeing in the blackness.

Visions drifted around her. A white-haired man, his beautiful armor caked with gore.

"You are going to die," he said, in a voice neither cruel nor kind. His accent was unfamiliar, his cadence plain and quick. "It has tainted you. The change will be worse than you can imagine."

He held a small vial filled with green-blue water above her and unstoppered it. In all the haze, in all the dark, his movements looked fluid and slow at once. "I can give you peace."

She wanted to nod. Wanting wasn't enough to make it happen.

"Or I can give you time. Years. Decades. Perhaps longer."

Alodie's body felt like it was drifting somewhere far away. She could barely hear the words. But they held her attention.

He continued, his pitch rising. "It will not be easy. You will train, and you will hunt. And you will die a monster, more wretched than the one that took your life. Your end will be no better for the evil you have slain, for all the good you have done."

The good you have done. She tried to look around for Linn. Failed at it.

Urgent words transfixed her. "If you would wake to this life, then vow. Vow it on your blood."

Alodie was unable to speak. Unable to move. She let her eyes answer him.

INSTINCTS

The ritual was hurried. Chanting and ablutions from the vial, the darkness of the cave sinking its fingers into Alodie's eyes like a thing alive. She lapsed in and out of consciousness, spoke, listened, remembered only pieces.

Standing turned out to be a labor, but she stood. Breathed. Ran her tongue over her teeth. Normal. Felt her pulse. Blood beating still. Looked at the white-haired man sitting cross-legged a few feet from her.

Between them was a small puddle of dew. Alodie realized she could see in the dark. Naturally, as she'd done so many times, she checked her reflection.

The wound on her throat was an ugly stitch. Her eyes glinted like light through rubies. They were surrounded by tiny veins the color of grave dirt.

She felt the pang of irreversible change, and let it go. The first need was to live. The second—

Linn sat up as though she had been dragged. Her arms hung limply at her sides. Her face was sallow. Spines poked through the skin of her neck and arms. A guttural, animal noise rose in her throat.

Somehow, Alodie felt weaker than she ever had.

"What you did to me," Alodie told Zebediah, stammering over the words, "do it for her. You have to."

Zebediah shook his head. "She has progressed too far. She will be a thrall of the vampire soon. I am sorry. I only had time for one of you."

All Alodie had left was the good she could do. He had said that. He had made it a promise.

"We . . . If we kill the vampire, will she . . ." Her voice sounded raspier than she remembered, as if her throat hadn't healed right.

Zebediah cut in. "Once the change takes hold in earnest, there is no stopping it."

Alodie felt sick. Tears came unbidden to her eyes, the same useless leaking they'd always been.

"Why me? Why didn't you pick her?"

Zebediah looked away. "Ours is a hard road, and you must know who you are to walk it. Forget yourself—even for a moment—and there is no way back." There was a far-off look in his eyes as he turned back to her. "I sense that resolution in you. You, at least, have a chance."

She walked to Linn, who was writhing like the puppet bodies at the carriage. Trying to get closer to Alodie with arms and legs that wouldn't listen. Making sounds that weren't quite words.

Alodie looked in her eyes, watched her pupils as they turned red and spread out, eclipsing the whites.

Linn couldn't say anything back to her. And nothing was worth saying just to herself.

The sumptuous blue-and-gold ascot around Linn's neck was stained to unrecognizability. Alodie slowly unwound it, pulled it over her head, and tied it around her neck, covering the scar. Her own keepsake.

She looked back at Zebediah. Not asking. Accepting. He handed her his spear.

Alodie pointed the spear at Linn's heart. Waited for some kind of a reaction. For trust to show in Linn's eyes. Mercifully, she didn't see it.

Trust.

She closed her eyes and let the instincts push.

We Are All Guilty

A SHORT STORY BY

RYAN QUINN

WE ARE ALL GUILTY

When they marched Kez out of her cell and onto the barge, silence harried her more than two years in a cage. Nobody shoved, spat, or flung rotted fish or words twice as spoilt. Guards in wide saw-scale helmets slow-walked her up the slippery plank, one hand each on her shoulders, steady but gentle as the good rain.

It had been different last time. Last time she deserved it.

But today they needed her, she figured. So there was respect, or what little of it these lampreys could fake. If she was lucky, they'd let her eat with her hands instead of chin-down in a bowl.

The end of her atonement was so overdue, Kez was surprised anyone had bothered. Maybe her accuser was dead. Maybe they were just going for a swim. She didn't let herself hope it was anything more than a break in the storm.

Kez stepped around the square turquoise sail and onto the back bench of the barge her escort appointed her to.

It was a gray day, which meant dripping rain and numb faces, but no hail. Kez filled her lungs with icy, bracing air. There were figures lumped all over the back bench and down in the rows, breath preceding them in the cold, a few peering over when she came aboard. A motley of pales and tans, talls and shorts, made uniform in haphazardly stitched brown prisoners' clothes.

Their arms were covered, but they had no furs; some shivered and huddled together like she'd done with the neighbors back home when it got too cold to be alone. Home was Rag Sound, westernmost of the Cold Isles, one of the many tiny islets surrounding the capital of Pelghain. Tiny islets draped in a skirt of flotsam from the city's ports, always last to hear of a crisis until the waves dropped it on top of them. Home was Rag Sound before home was the cage.

One of the prisoners, a thick-neck with a pig's nose and retreating black hair, was coughing and moving his throat like he'd swallowed a squid. But he paused at the sight of Kez, snorted up something, shook his head, and looked over at the guards.

"Just lovely. Anyone else you need me to carry on my back? A baby, perhaps?"

He hacked a couple more times. Kez took him for a hunter,

maybe—she could see him out in the swells with a horn and a spear to feed his family. Nobody special. Probably sent to the cage after a fistfight in view of the wrong people.

Kez knew what he saw when he looked back at her.

Dusky skin, dark hair so unkempt it flew free of her hood and billowed in the wind even wet. Wiry, but shorter than most. Hands at her sides, her feet pointed away from each other as if she were preparing to jump. The cage hadn't taken that from her—couldn't—even when there wasn't room to stand. Her prison clothes were frayed; the neck and hems looked like rats had been at them.

Kez did not cough or shiver much in the cold. Only her lip wriggled like a thing clinging to life. Her brows pinched together. She could show this thick-neck he was wrong, could take him to the ground and let the other scabs laugh at him. He was here for atonement, after all.

But that wouldn't get her home.

Instead, she tried to remember what she could of the training. Imagined herself in the middle of a ring of people, all whispering and shouting at her, all wanting things she couldn't possibly give them, contradictory things. A storm of distractions. Needs that were beyond her. Needs she had to let go. She listened to them scream until it sounded like a hum.

The furrows in Kez's brow eased. She relaxed her lips until they were a straight line, betraying nothing. Her face became a mask of simple placidity. Calm was just another prison, but she needed to pretend. Even so, Kez tapped her manacled wrists on the rail of the barge. She couldn't help it. Two years. Two *shit* years. She'd been shut away long enough to waste all that promise the sages had talked about. But she didn't say a thing aloud in rebuttal. Just tapped and listened to the hunter cough until he glanced away.

Then she heard the squeak of boots coming up the plank. Solid boots, not sealskin. An officious stride, in perfect step with others. Wind howled in her ears—just hers; the sails of the barge lay utterly still. Her throat closed of its own accord.

Three guards banged their spear hafts on the deck. One intoned, "Sage Kynon," and each of the others repeated it in turn, matching their volume.

Kez flexed her hands, doing her best not to look at him.

Kynon was dressed imperially, in the style of old Pelghain. A pair of dyed red-and-purple wool mantles crisscrossed his shoulders, held together by a golden clasp of two scepters. Thick hair unspooled around his throat and shoulders, though he kept a trim beard.

His mouth was tranquil and downturned, his eyes gray and—coupled with the frown—pathetic.

The look of a functionary. An empty vessel. Only his station demanded attention.

Even with her hands manacled, Kez was sure she could charge him and knock them both off the barge. Maybe he'd gash his head

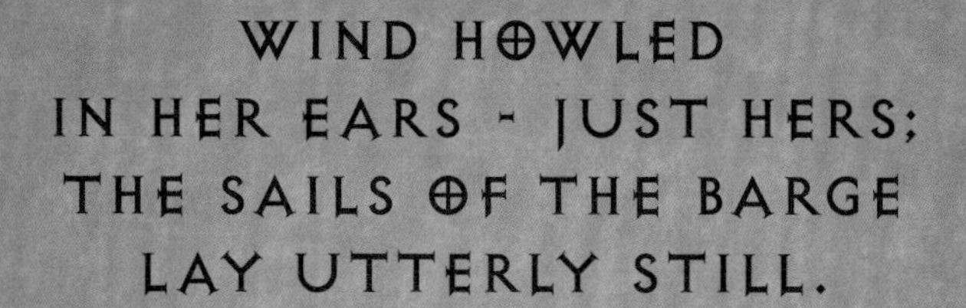

WIND HOWLED
IN HER EARS - JUST HERS;
THE SAILS OF THE BARGE
LAY UTTERLY STILL.

HER THROAT CLOSED
OF ITS OWN ACCORD.

on the plank as he fell. Maybe the maarozhi—sea beasts—would be on him before he could swim back.

Her constant companion since the training—the ring of voices from her mind and her heart, which sounded like her and her old friends and a hundred ancient whispers she hadn't named—burbled for calm. *Wind is not cut,* they said. *Waves are not stopped. Find tranquility in the heart of the storm, and such tranquility endures its passing.*

She shut them out. She couldn't even *feign* calm, hearing the mists whisper to her like this.

Kynon paced in front of the back bench. One of the prisoners, a gangly sort with sopping brown hair, sat up straighter as the sage's eyes passed over him. Kynon ignored him and spoke, cheeks puffing like a fish.

"Mehrwen's Stay is an islet of little import or travel. This week it is drowned in the mists."

Kez knew the Stay. A half day's sail from Rag Sound. Named for—supposedly—serving as a onetime retreat for Mehrwen, the moralizing and dour empress of old. The mists, most of the sages insisted, were Mehrwen's last breath, when she swam away from her murderous sister to die somewhere people could still find and praise her.

The sage continued. "We were able to evacuate most of the people. Not all. If any who remained behind rose as fiends, they must be put to rest. Else, when the winds shift . . . they will journey upon them." Straight through Rag Sound and the rest of the isles to slaughter folk, if history was any indication.

Kynon read the prisoners' names and numbers, one at a time. Ponnyd, Cedrouk, Silla. All from the same isle.

"Gart, from Rag Sound. One year of atonement. One year remaining." The hunter with the pig nose hacked in answer.

"Only one?" someone else whispered, incredulous.

Gart smirked.

Kynon ignored them. "Paltik, from Rag Sound. Four months of atonement. One year remaining." Paltik was the one who'd sat straight up when Kynon looked at him. He saluted at Kynon's back as the sage paced.

"Kez, from Rag Sound," he said, with no more or less emotion than the others. "Two years of atonement. Two years remaining."

"Yes," was all she said.

"Though you have failed in your duty to your station, Pelghain does not see your flaws today. Only your promise." He sounded tired, like he'd given this speech before.

"Your atonement is no longer to hold yourself apart, but to try again." He gestured to all of them, though his gaze remained on her. "To honor your guilt and to prove that your souls have been changed by it. You do this in two days' time, and I will annul your sentence. You will be free to dwell in any of the refuge isles as will have you."

Two days. Then home. It sunk in deep.

Kynon paused, plainly for effect. "Should you fail and somehow survive, you will return to your cages and hide your shame from the sky."

Kez decided not to tackle him. No one got off the boat.

Gart's coughing eased over the journey, as they closed in on the islet of Mehrwen's Stay. The barge, big enough to seat the sage's entire retinue, needed a lot of hands, and Kynon ordered the prisoners' manacles removed so they could row. After he marched out of sight, Kez wondered, not for the first time, if they might revolt. Take over the barge and sail for . . . somewhere else. It would have to be well beyond the storms. And farther than any of them had sailed in their lives.

But she understood the allure of atonement after all these years. Two days and a bit of dark work, and they'd all be home. And she knew the spines of people like Paltik, with his fast salutes—they didn't know how to refuse an opportunity. They were from Rag Sound. Most of them had never known opportunity of any kind.

The mists were settling in around them, sticking like ice-white cobwebs to the barge's netting, placed to keep out sleet but worthless against the murk. Near the prow, someone was blasting a sounding horn on a steady cadence. When the mists fell, it was easier to collide with quiet things.

A few of the Rag Sounders had jostled together to get oars

and push the barge for the first leg of the journey. As the day lengthened, their pace slowed until Kynon signaled for the guards to row the rest of the way.

The Sounders were rude clay, but Gart at least seemed like he'd been in a fight. Kez shifted over to where he was speaking with Paltik and cleared her throat.

"Did the sage or guards say how many to expect? Anything about the land? What weapons they brought for us?"

Gart laughed out loud. "You giving orders now?"

Kez knew his type. There was only one authority in his world, so she appealed. "No. I'm trying to make sure we get out of this alive."

He stood up, steady despite the ground wobbling. Gart was tall—the kind who loomed simply by being near. He cracked his knuckles; it sounded like he did it often.

He didn't have a weapon on him. Not that she could see. But he had reach, and his fists were free after too long bound up. Kez tried to keep her placidity in place as he sneered down at her. "Don't play at telling me what to do, girl."

Calm was not helping, but Kez didn't want to hurt their slim chances. She struggled to tamp down her irritation. "I've been to the Spiral and back. You're lucky I'm telling you what to do."

Gart smiled at that, all gap teeth, his hog face taking on a manic cast as he stepped closer to her and spread his arms wide. The message was clear: *You're just talking. Come on. Take a swing.* If the

"KYNON DOESN'T
TELL US ANYTHING
BECAUSE HE DOESN'T CARE
IF PEOPLE FROM RAG SOUND
LIVE OR DIE. BUT I DO. AND I
CAN GET US HOME."

GART WAS DEATHLY
QUIET, SO KEZ KEPT
ON. "I PROMISE. ON
THE SOUND."

guards could see them squaring up, they paid them no mind.

Kez couldn't throw Gart off the barge. He'd freeze to death. So she rose to a standing position, pointed a fist at him, and yanked back her other arm for a body blow. Gart tensed, raised his guard—and she kicked him right in the yoke.

It was a cheap shot, a Rag Sound special. Hazardous and familiar. Small chaos followed, with gangly Paltik struggling to hold back the other prisoners, a few ready to fling her off the barge and most laughing so hard they forgot they were cold.

Though the veins in Gart's neck bulged out, once he regained his composure he started laughing too. Kez held her hands up to show she was done. She kept her voice loud enough for the Sounders to hear, if not the sage's people.

"Kynon doesn't tell us anything because he doesn't care if people from Rag Sound live or die. But I do. And I can get us home."

Gart was deathly quiet, so Kez kept on.

"I promise. On the Sound."

Gart stood, hocked something over the side of the barge, and held his hands up. Smiling different now. Listening to her at last.

Kez, Gart, and Paltik eased their way over to the front of the barge, stepping carefully as patches of fog drifted down all around them. Two from Kynon's retinue flanked him for protection; another sat on a massive trunk, occasionally blowing a horn to signal their way through the mist. The sage was looking intently past the prow, but he turned swiftly when Kez spoke up.

"How many are there?"

Kynon was grim. "We evacuated all but two families. There should be no more than eight souls left on land."

They were six prisoners in total, by Kez's count. Ponnyd, Cedrouk, Silla, Paltik, Gart, and herself. She stepped closer to Kynon, careful not to enter what his guards might consider threatening range.

"Where are your Tempests?"

He cocked an eyebrow at that. It wasn't the question he'd expected from her, of all people.

"*They* are needed at Pelghain. *You* are the closest thing to a Tempest in reach of Mehrwen's Stay," he said flatly.

Gart scoffed, heedless of what it meant to question a sage's words. "She's really a Tempest?" He looked at her with disbelief and something new. Fear? Admiration?

Kez started to say that she would be by now, but Kynon slashed her protests to pieces. "She was in *training*. And she is lucky to carry Mehrwen's burdens still."

She *had* finished most of the training. Had drifted across icy lakes alone, drinking the mists in, minutes at a time, for years. Had learned the blade dance, slain maarozhi, had even paid the cost to command the wind and waves, to become a vessel for the wisdom of Pelghain's past. She'd inherited a lifetime of incessant words in her mind, centuries of recollection in a thousand different voices.

Irritability had always come easily to Kez—but the mists, the constant soft buzz of their whispers, made it worse. Calm was her nation's highest pursuit for good reason.

Her status was not up for discussion. Not with him. "What's in the trunk?"

The guard with the horn dutifully hopped off the trunk and flipped it open. "Spears for all of you. Some sturdy leathers."

"And?" Kez waited for more, and when she didn't hear it, she kept up. "Where's my sword?"

Kynon sighed. "It will be useless to you."

So he had it. Had he brought it to remind her of her failure?

Anger at a sage was serious; loud anger was punishable. Kez tried to form the right words, to entreat him. But all that came out was her pain.

"That's years of my life, you cawing shit."

Kynon's fish cheeks bulged. He raised both his arms, and his retinue stepped forward. The guard with the horn looked like she might grab Kez, but Kez tensed her hands into fists and bent her knees.

Paltik jabbed Kez in the kidneys as he stepped between them. His meaning was clear: *If one of us makes trouble, all of us go in the water.* A lackey's way.

"Sage Kynon, please, I beg you listen. She forgets herself . . . but she speaks for each of our atonements." Paltik pointed at himself with a soft palm, pointed at Kez, the guards, the other prisoners, the sage. "Please. We are all guilty."

Kez *hated* that phrase. It was commonplace in every corner of the Cold Isles, no matter how far from Pelghain. It meant, "Remember that everyone makes mistakes," but also "Everyone is responsible for everyone else's mistakes." The worst kind of cowardice—spreading out the blame for something *you* did, until there was so little left nobody could see it. It led the weak to leadership, forgave the unforgivable . . . and it played favorites. Kynon's guilt—the sages' guilt—belonged to every soul in the Cold Isles, but Kez's anger was her problem. No matter how right it felt.

Paltik's words worked for Sage Kynon, though. Of course. He shook his head. "Have it, then."

The guards opened the trunk and dug around while he continued. "I will return tomorrow at sunset. Do not address me until you have proof the fiends' numbers are thinned. With at least one slain for each of you, or your atonement will continue."

As the others slipped on boiled leathers, a guard placed Kez's sword in her hands, and she fought back a sigh. She remembered when its sawteeth broke. Nobody had bothered to fix it. At least the metal was polished enough to reflect her face.

A wind edge was supposed to be precious, a blade that let Tempests harness the fury of the northern gales against Pelghain's enemies. This one's hilt was years from a fitting. It was an old, pitted thing, in the worst shape it had ever been.

But not useless. Not to her.

WE ARE ALL GUILTY

They hopped off the barge at the flattest part of a rocky brown expanse, ringed with drifting crusts of ice large enough to raft on. A dell split the islet's hills down the middle, where the mists would be thickest, and six prisoners trudged toward it with Kez in the lead.

Kynon had told Gart—because he refused to address Kez directly—that he would not wait near the mists for their work to be done. He was needed elsewhere, or so he claimed. And he asked that those unequal to the task wait on the shore for his return, rather than risk being killed and rising as mistfiends, worsening the threat.

They were warmer, at least. Kynon had given them furs, great dense cloaks of stinking, matted sheep's wool, and pouches of dried mushrooms. The sage had taken a passing interest in their success. But that didn't mean he needed them all to come back.

They paused for air at the side of the dell, the sound of their boots cracking gravel an odd substitute for the islet's absent birds and insects.

Through the valley's entrance, they could see white mist pouring upward from the ground like freezing breath. Clumps floated by their company, solid enough that Kez sidestepped to avoid touching them, and she urged the others to do the same. She'd seen untrained folk take in too much of the mists—gasping for air like they'd fallen into freezing water, their skin ice cold, suffocating before they rose as fiends. When the wind died and the brushing of the waves against stone faded into the distance, the mists writhed even still.

The contingent held their spears in a muddle of stances, some ahead with their elbows locked, some tight in at their sides. Kez wrinkled her nose at that. Maybe half of them had brought spears on a hunt. At most.

Paltik had his hands choked up on a spear when Kez tapped him on the shoulder and adjusted his grip. "You need enough room that you can stab something without getting your fingers near it."

"You should go in front, Paltik," Gart broke in, shaking his head at the display. "A man of the empire knows what he's good for."

Kez rounded on him. "Stop acting like you're the only one here. If any of us die, the fiends' numbers grow. Simple enough for you to see the problem?"

Gart just snickered. At least he'd shut up. Paltik was certainly ashamed, but she caught him shifting his grip as they walked, taking practice jabs at the air.

It wasn't much. But it was something, and she had promised on Rag Sound itself to protect them. So she plodded on, looking back and forth between the path and the blade of her sole sword, checking her reflection every few minutes to see that the mists hadn't entirely closed around her group.

The people of Mehrwen's Stay would have built their houses

SHE'D SEEN
UNTRAINED FOLK
TAKE IN TOO MUCH OF
THE MISTS—GASPING FOR
AIR LIKE THEY'D FALLEN
INTO FREEZING WATER.

THEIR SKIN ICE COLD,
SUFFOCATING BEFORE
THEY ROSE AS FIENDS.

high up, out of the dell, to avoid flooding. Kez reasoned that the Sounders might climb the valley's ridge and search for their quarry in their former homes. She led the prisoners upslope in wide arcs, zigzagging away from the valley walls whenever they grew fog laden, testing piles of loose gravel herself before urging the others forward.

She had hoped the mists would be thinner as they ascended, but nearly an hour in, Cedrouk and Silla were starting at sounds Kez missed, jerking their heads around painfully fast and mumbling to themselves. A sure sign.

Kez piped up, precise with instructions but silent on the consequences. "I'm going to talk, and I'm not going to stop until we get somewhere clearer. I want you to listen to my voice and ignore everything else you hear."

No one argued as she drove them steeply uphill, yammering about the Sound, about ice walks on the flats and the last good bowl of sattlefin and mushroom she could remember before atonement, and even things she didn't like talking about, like missing her friends back home.

"Shircan and I used to go ice walking out on the flats in summer. I don't think she wanted to be a Tempest. But when you see parts of your home breaking off and floating away . . ."

You have to do something. She didn't say it, but Paltik nodded anyway.

"We begged the sages to teach us the blade dance. We lay out on the ice, told them every pure and dark thing in our hearts. I thought by the third day they would say we weren't good enough and send us home. But they didn't. They judged us fair back then. I practiced for months until they let us row out to the Spiral. It took years before our first sip of the mists. We . . ."

She trailed off. She had to stay calm. Had to focus.

"You was doing what, before all that?" Gart asked, huffing along.

"Just scavving. Trying to keep the roof on." Nothing special.

"Oh yeah? Me too," he said.

"Same," Paltik said.

When she ran out of things to talk about, Kez started to repeat the prayers of purification, of calm, of legacy—three at a time, just saying them aloud, not thinking about what they meant.

Power uncontrolled is the doom of the soul.

To live in the sight of others is to change.

Great works rinse small rancor.

Paltik repeated them with her, and some of the others took them up, though they still shot uneasy glances around. Halfway up the side of the dell, the mists wrapped around clumps of snowy rock, pointing up and out like a jumble of fingers.

They were fine until they weren't. Kez checked her reflection again, and she couldn't even see herself for all the shrouding. She held up a hand to halt them.

The others looked terrified. Kez had trained in places like this one, but she'd started with minutes at a time. Even full-fledged

Tempests wouldn't chance mists like this, dense sheer walls pushing down on them from above.

The ridge wouldn't work.

If there was somewhere to hide deeper in the dell, down at the valley bottom, maybe her call could still reach their quarry. It was no longer raining, after all. The winds were calm. If they stayed that way, maybe the mists wouldn't settle on top of them.

That was it. If they could find a stream within a few minutes, they'd have cover, water, and an obstacle. If not, they would double back, take a long walk around, and try the ridge from the opposite side. Looking at Paltik's halting gait and Gart's manic glances around, Kez felt her choice making itself. She spoke loudly.

"I'm going to stop talking, and we're going to move fast. The *only* thing you need to listen for is the sound of a stream or a river. We find flowing water, and we head upstream."

No longer mouthy, Gart jogged to the front of the pack, jutting his head out to squint in the fog. "I got good ears. Let me take the lead."

She'd figured Gart for a hunter; he seemed like he knew what he was doing, so she didn't object. And the others ran behind him, heads swiveling as Kez did her best to listen for moving water and ignore the half-formed whispers creeping at her ears.

Power uncontrolled is the doom of the soul.

And then:

Power gripped tight is the doom of the world.

They scurried quickly down the hill, lungs sore from half

breaths. As the valley flattened out and their trail started to wind, they kept a tight line behind Gart, stone silent, making sure none could be lost to the mists.

Gart stopped so short Kez almost ran into him. His shoulders were squared, and he was staring at something she couldn't see. Kez tensed, backed up a couple steps, moving her sword in front of her body as he turned—

And he was chuckling, standing a few dozen feet from a sluggish, half-frozen turquoise stream, empty of fish and plants. The water crawled over angular rocks a few feet deep, but Kez could see it widening further off, perhaps a minute's run from the valley wall. It might work.

Her sigh of relief frosted out, and similar gusts followed from the other silhouettes around her. Their features were hard to see, even as they fanned out and came nearer. She counted. Five others. All the prisoners were here.

"The people who died will come for us if we make ourselves known," Kez explained. "I'm going to use this stream and call just one of them."

She continued. "Some look like they did when they were alive. But they're not people anymore. They're fiends of the mists. They'll take your breath and your skin if you let them."

Paltik's face twisted in horror, and Kez reflexively put a finger to her lips. Gart, uncharacteristically quiet, asked if she'd ever killed any.

KEZ HELD HER
SWORD IN A REVERSE
GRIP, THE BLADE CURVING
ALONG HER ARM, AND WEAVED
IT LIKE SHE WAS PAINTING.

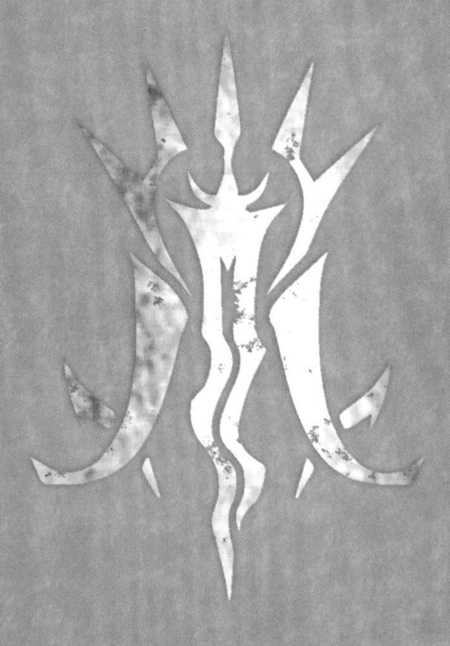

THE AIR WAS HER
PALETTE AND CANVAS.
MIST DRIFTED AROUND
THE EDGE IN THIN,
UNNATURAL RIBBONS.

"Not yet," she said. "But I've seen them die."

"That why you only have the one sword?" Gart asked, snickering at his own joke. Tempests bore two, as a matter of both pride and pragmatism.

Kez was learning to ignore his barbs.

She looked at Paltik. "Listen to me. We can make it out of here, and then that sage won't have any hold over us ever again."

"How do you know?" He sounded tentative. On the brink of something.

"I promised," she said, with more heat than she'd wanted, but repeating herself was a waste of breath. "I promised on the Sound, didn't I?"

He didn't say anything, just looked at her, so she pushed on. "We can ambush them, and we can kill them. One at a time, if we're careful. You just need to do exactly what I say."

No one protested, so Kez told them everything she knew about what would happen next.

"To reach them, I need this water to flow," Kez said, gesturing at the ice-clogged stream, "as fast as possible."

Rag Sound did not boast the elevated cave networks of Old Pinnacle or the mighty seawalls of Stormbrace. But everyone on the Sound knew how to scavenge, how to break things down, though it did no good to the legacy of imperial Pelghain. So the prisoners found heavy, oblong stones in a matter of minutes, brought them in a hurried line, and hurled them into the stream to shatter the ice.

Kez held her sword in a reverse grip, the blade curving along her arm, and weaved it like she was painting. The air was her palette and canvas. Mist drifted around the edge in thin, unnatural ribbons. The prisoners looked to her in formation, and she spoke her best wisdom to them.

"They're drawn to our breath. Take a deep one. Don't breathe in any of the mist. When I say, Gart and Paltik, push out everything in your lungs. The rest of you, hold it. Keep your spears at hand. It'll happen fast."

As her contingent sucked in air, Kez rolled up her sleeve and ran the ragged edge of her sword across her underarm. It bit painfully, but she got what she needed. A dozen drops of blood, barely visible, fell into the icy stream. She watched the water flow, pointing her stained sword at it, willing to dead Mehrwen that it would be fast enough.

And it was. Ice cracked as the wind whipped where Kez's blade aimed, the stream surging forth, carrying her blood to the heart of the Stay.

"Now."

Gart and Paltik expelled frosty breath into the air. Seconds later, as if in response, a solitary keening answered, a canine snarl delivered as a human scream. Closer than anyone expected. Kez's call had worked too well.

They barely had time to scoop up their spears as the mists washed over them like a tide.

Kez twisted, trying to keep her eyes in the present as phantoms from her past reached for her mind.

Soldiers yelled for their families as they waited to die. Sage Kynon shouted at them to keep fighting. Somehow, she could hear each voice, clear over the impossibly loud crashing of the ocean. It was violent, not today's calm. And those people weren't her comrades. Weren't *these* comrades.

Everything in the mists was unmoored in time. They held memory inside and craved more, and Kez was out of practice at keeping them back.

So she bit her cheek, hard enough to make it bleed, and held tightly to her sword and swung. She found herself in the present again, mist rushing around her feet and billowing over her eyes like a wet blindfold.

Kez spun in a circle, commanding the wind to carry the mists away, and they did as she bade, whirling back from her outstretched sword. She couldn't disperse all the mists, but maybe she could hold them at bay.

In the ringing clouds, she looked for the others, but saw only two forms come into focus: Paltik and the shadow devouring him.

The mistfiend had been a girl about half Kez's age not long ago. Death in the mists had dyed its loose braids the color of old moss. Its skin was etiolated and its eyes gaunt, with nails longer than fingers. Its jaw was stretched stiff in anguish, and its eyes were empty as a corpse's. The mist was its puppeteer.

Kez had told Paltik, had told all of them, not to attack before the fiend was fully manifest. But his spear lay on the ground, and the mistfiend's cold fingers were clamped around his wrist and throat.

Kez couldn't keep the mists back and strike at it. But as long as it held a living being, it was briefly form and flesh. And Paltik, bless him, was screaming loud enough for everyone to hear.

She shouted for the rest of them.

Two spears flashed from the whirling mists, and then another, and another. Cedrouk stabbed the arm that held Paltik's wrist. Gart tore the mistfiend's leg from under it, and it looked back at him with that unmoving, agonized dead face as two more spears crossed through its sides. It died soundlessly, white mist leaking from its empty eyes.

Kez spun, searching for more fiends. She saw none.

Summoning a heavy breeze, she cleared the air around Paltik. The skin about his left wrist and throat looked like dried rheum, peeling and sloughing off where the fiend had grabbed him. He looked at Kez, let out a wet, shuddering cough that made his whole body convulse, and crumpled to the ground.

And there he breathed. Steadily. Alive.

The mists whistled around them in a perfect circle as Kez held her control. The wind was hers, and it was moving.

"Five more?" Paltik wheezed. "We should go back to the shore."

"Only need four more if you get yourself killed," Gart said.

If they lingered on the shore too long, the maarozhi would show. They always did. Kez didn't fancy fighting the dead and sea beasts at once. She shook her head.

Besides, they had done it. She'd done it. Paltik pulled himself along the ground toward the mistfiend, its skin flowing like ink. He wriggled a worn bronze anklet off its foot before pocketing it as proof.

Kez thought about who the mistfiend girl had been. She tried to imagine what Mehrwen's Stay might have looked like before the mists, or even further back, before the storms rose to torment old Pelghain. Would children dare each other to walk out onto the ice flats and come home safe? Would people build houses fearlessly under the sky, unafraid of the deluge and things from the deep?

If she finished her training, if she caught up to her promise, maybe then she could help make it real.

Kez opened her eyes, shaking off the reveries that came so easily here. The mists had curled along the ground as Kez relaxed, and they wheeled around the prisoners' legs. The valley had seemed calm earlier, but with all the wind she'd called down . . .

"We're going to higher ground." Her voice was more frantic than she'd wanted it to be. She yelled at Gart. "Help him. I'll bring up the rear and shove the mists back."

"Up the ridge again?" Paltik asked. He was wobbly on his feet.

Mist trickled, falling softly from above. Tiny wisps and flakes now, but soon—

"I'm not carrying him," Gart shouted, directly at Kez, then looked around at the others. "If you'd like to, have at it!"

Kez was unyielding. "We're not leaving him behind. Besides, he can still hold a spear. Can't you, Paltik?"

Paltik nodded. Unsteady. Good enough.

Gart crossed his arms and planted his feet, digging in to waste more time arguing. Then the mists settled atop them both, like a blanket draped over the valley floor, and he vanished from her sight.

Kez twirled her blade to try to save them, carving a tunnel of empty air in the direction of the valley wall, but it wasn't half as wide as she'd expected. She felt the mists enfolding her, pressing in on her from all sides, with a weight impossible for how they moved.

"Run! The ridge!" she screamed.

She had no chance to see if they made it.

The mists washed over Kez, drowning her in memory.

Kez was still yelling after the people she'd lost. They couldn't hear her over the din.

The waves boomed and the wind roared, and the snarling of the maarozhi cut through it anyway. Two years ago, the unstoppable storms had sent waves smashing into Rag Sound, and the sea beasts rode them onto the islet as it flooded.

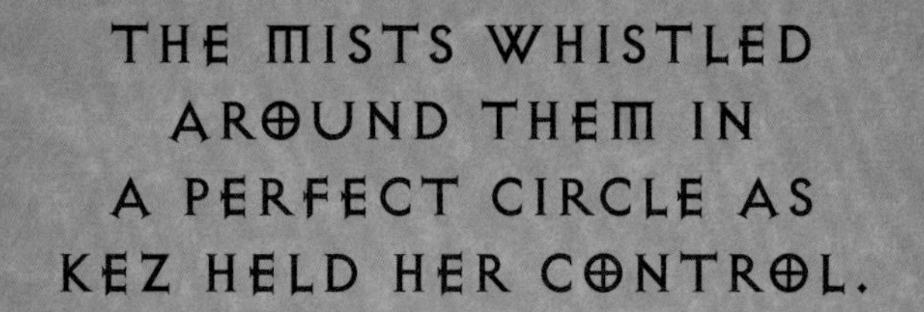

THE WIND WAS HERS,
AND IT WAS MOVING.

Rag Sound's seawall was not like the glorious edifice shielding Pelghain, festooned in teal and white and decorated by artists and amateurs from every part of the capital. Rag Sound's seawall was made of the same stuff as its people—leftovers.

*But Kez had her orders. When the storm began to pound and rage, Sage Kynon came down from the cavetops, from high dwellings spared the worst of the flooding. He gathered Rag Sound's handful of bladedancers, Tempests in training, to tell them there would be no help from Pelghain, that they—*they*—were their home's last line of defense.*

The sage put his charges in two groups—two bladedancers and a half dozen militia volunteers for the stilt homes of her neighborhood, to protect the new arrivals who by bad fortune or bad choice ended up near the coast, away from the safety of the cavetops.

And all the remaining militia and eight bladedancers, Kez included, for the seawall.

Kez swore that they had more than enough to hold the seawall, that the division was a disaster, but the sage brooked no argument. A seawall was Rag Sound's survival as it was survival for every spit of land in the Cold Isles. And Rag Sound was part of the legacy of imperial Pelghain. And Pelghain was its generations past and future, much more than it was the people living today.

So Kez went to battle, clambered down the swaying miscellany of the seawall, waves smashing all around her, and hewed into the maarozhi until her clothes were black with their blood and her fingernails and most of her sword's teeth had broken on their scales.

She didn't fight alone. It likely saved her life. Kez fell more than once, cracked herself head to tail on the wreck of the wall, only to be lifted gently to her feet by summoned wind. Shircan, whom she'd known since girlhood, strode on the tips of her toes across the wreckage, holding a wind edge in her right hand and a practice blade in her left. She needed to wield both blades, like a real Tempest, for balance, she had said.

Shircan died slumped against the wall, with a maarozh tail spine in her throat and a brown line of bile clinging to her chin.

Moon-eyed Izavel sprang between the maarozhi like lightning, her elegant whips of water shearing their limbs free. Until a colossus with the body of a great shark and a ripping lamprey mouth bore her down to the rocks at the seawall's base and pulled her to pieces in a moment.

Kez wept and fought with her eyes closed for hour-length minutes. She slipped and picked herself up more times than she could count, let the enemy constrict her close so she could tear their underbellies open with wind honed to razors. The seawall did not break, though the monsters ripped at it, though Kez shook with fever and every part of her burned when at last she climbed from the melee.

Scores of wriggling maarozhi bodies lay sticky and gull-eaten along the jagged breakwater. And for the moment, Rag Sound held.

Atop the seawall, Kynon and his retinue watched her climb, and the sage even extended a hand to pull her up, not flinching at the blood. He looked glum but unsurprised, like he hadn't expected any other outcome. Like he'd paid slightly too much for a nice sattlefish at market.

"YOU USED THEM."
"THEY FOUGHT TO THE BEST OF THEIR ABILITY. THEY BOUGHT US TIME TO DEFEND OUR GREATEST ASSET."
"YOU WASTED THEIR LIVES!"

SHE POINTED AN ACCUSING FINGER AT THE SAGE. "WE ARE ALL GUILTY," KYNON SAID. THAT WAS THE END OF IT.

Kez didn't waste a second. There was still time, she yelled over the booming storm. They had the seawall in hand. They should divert every soul they could spare to the coast.

"The coast is lost," Kynon shouted back. "We need you here. Should the storms shift, the maarozhi could rise again and overwhelm us."

Kynon had picked his choke point, marshaled his forces to it. And decided what he was willing to lose to keep it. So many of her friends and neighbors gone, but the lands of the dying empire endured.

Below them, the hair and cloaks of Rag Sound's defenders swished lifelessly in the ocean.

For what? It was too much.

"Why send any to the coast? Why not just order the residents to higher ground, rally the defenders here?"

"Focus is your enemy's most precious resource. And even a single bladedancer can split the focus of the maarozhi."

There it was. So plain. Spoken as if she were a child.

"You used them."

"They fought to the best of their ability. They bought us time to defend our greatest asset."

"You wasted their lives!" She pointed an accusing finger at the sage.

"We are all guilty," Kynon said.

That was the end of it.

She punched Kynon in the jaw hard enough to knock him to the ground, screaming like an animal while his retinue pulled her back and clamped her in manacles. So began her atonement.

Assaulting a sage should have meant exile. Or death. In Pelghain, there were many creative ways to combine the two. If Kynon thought she was worth killing, he'd have seen her tied to a raft the same day, drifting along the glacial flats near Shiver Cay, covered in offal, with a long, open cut down her belly. She'd spend the night with the seabirds at her entrails and be in a maarozh's stomach by sunrise.

But he had stuck her in the cage instead. And then let her out. Kynon, the cold fish, thought her life had value. In service to him.

Rag Sound was an isle of wreckage. Inclement and indefensible, a weave rotten to the weft. But Kez had bled for it.

What was any of it for if she didn't get home?

Kez felt like she'd been punched in the jaw herself.

In the mists, the past bore into now. She'd scrambled halfway up the ridge of Mehrwen's Stay when she was climbing the seawall in her memories, following screams she could still hear. Screams she *knew*. She'd moved slower than the Sounders, lost in her reverie. And because of that . . .

The mists weren't gone this high up, but they were thinner. Freed from their eddying, Kez came back to herself. Her hands were bitten and bruised from grabbing the rocks, but her sword was still at her side.

Kez raced the rest of the way, the wind buoying her every step, carrying her off her feet as she scrabbled from rock to rock and neared the hilltop in minutes. Most of the prisoners' screams had quieted by then, and she dreaded finding them with lungs full of mist. Another ill-fated battle she'd somehow survived.

She summited the ridge and stood on a mercifully flat outcropping. Mist whirled around her feet. Testing. Not devouring. She would not have to mind it as she had in the valley.

Forms drifted across the hilltop, most trailing smoke behind them. Four mistfiends crowded around Gart. He had slumped to the ground, his arms limp. One fiend's drifting remnants lay beneath him, but others crouched atop him, fighting to pull the warm breath from his lungs.

Two more fiends encircled Paltik, their fog-tipped fingers pushing into his skin through the earlier wounds he'd suffered. He was struggling to get away from them, but his spear was nowhere to be seen.

Kez sent a quick gust of wind spiraling out to disperse the remaining mist, to see if the fiends would follow it, but they were too intent on their prey.

They had barely defeated a single fiend with everyone standing. Now unarmed Paltik had to deal with two.

Still she would fight with everything she had.

Kez breathed out hard, and the nearest mistfiend, a tall farmer in the remains of a long tunic, broke away from Gart and lunged for her. Kez brought her sword around in a circle, and currents of air trapped the fiend inches from her face. She slashed her blade through it three times, preternaturally quick, and watched the rents she cut in the creature billow white clouds. This fiend had a simple pendant around its neck, and as it staggered Kez cut through the pendant's cord and yanked it to her. Another proof of death.

She sent flowing air through her sword and directly into the fiend drawing out Gart's breath, pitching herself forward and slamming into it with the force of a hurricane. Its body withered, swept away by the wheeling mists—but as Kez rose to her feet, the rest of the fiends raked her with taloned fingers, carving chunks from her flesh.

Kez danced back from them before they could drag her to the ground. The rents they'd left on her skin burned icy cold.

Gart's eyes were open now, but one wheezing mistfiend was still intent on him, and one had raced away from Paltik. It lurched for her with clenching hands, and she hacked it down frantically, vision narrowed to a pinpoint, not seeing another creeping from behind until it rose, tearing at her scalp and neck.

She gasped, first with the pain and then for breath as it tugged at her. Kez leaped away, letting the wind push when her seizing muscles failed to respond. It couldn't carry her far. Her control was floundering.

Shame and fury battered Kez as she glanced at her comrades. She'd let this happen to them. She had promised, and she was getting them all killed.

Kez swung her sword in an arc with her right hand to keep the fiend searching for an opening. She flung darts of air with her left, aiming for the creature surging around Paltik. It wouldn't be injured by a meager attack, but it might be distracted—and as the fiend turned from its prey, Kez blasted Paltik with a sweeping wind, tearing him free from its hands and dumping him on his back yards away. She saw him begin to stagger to his feet, and she retreated to the ridgeline as she looked around for Gart, exhausted.

She found him at the tree line. His face was ashen, unsmiling and wan. But he had downed one. He was a fighter. He might—

Sleepy-faced Cedrouk rose up right in front of Kez, fog gouting from his distended jaw. She whipped her sword harmlessly through his empty skull, let the blade fly from her hands, then flipped it back on air the moment he seized her. Cedrouk's head slipped from his neck, and his body slumped to the ground.

Yet Ponnyd and Silla crept dead-eyed on all fours behind him. The maarozhi were a scourge, but their numbers could be counted. The mistfiends grew in number with each life they took.

As she backed away, Kez's boots scraped gravel over the ridge.

Who was left to protect? Who had the best chance?

Gart was capable, but mortally wounded. The fiends were swarming Paltik, and he was breathing, but unlikely to slay another. The rest of the prisoners were either still or moving corpses. Kez was standing but ragged, her calls to the wind weakening as her life ebbed. Five fiends dead on the hilltop, yet still more remained. Kez knew they couldn't win.

They couldn't win.

The next words in her head came from a living voice, one from her own memory. *Focus is your enemy's most precious resource.*

And then: *They bought us time to defend our greatest asset.*

She *hated* that voice. But it was right.

Kez drew on every bit of faith and strength she had left. She clutched her blade in both hands, sent a dozen tendrils of wind spinning toward the surviving Sounders.

As Gart struggled to fight off two fiends with a sickly red hole spreading across his chest, the winds cradled him, too weak to lift him to his feet.

But strong enough to knock the air out of his lungs.

As he aspirated, dead Ponnyd and Silla turned from Kez, skeletal noses pointed to the sky, and saw easy prey. Kez stood shivering while the lost Sounders moved to feast.

Their hands closed around Gart's neck; their supping breaths pulled his life away. The fiends' hunger stirred, and they drew him down, and mist began to trickle into his mouth as it lolled open.

Paltik gasped madly, taking panicked sips of air that would not come. His frantic eyes searched for Kez, found her, met her by the ridgeline.

He was slumped to the ground, but she heard him over the hissing of the fiends.

THE NEXT WORDS IN HER HEAD CAME FROM A LIVING VOICE, ONE FROM HER OWN MEMORY. *FOCUS IS YOUR ENEMY'S MOST PRECIOUS RESOURCE.*

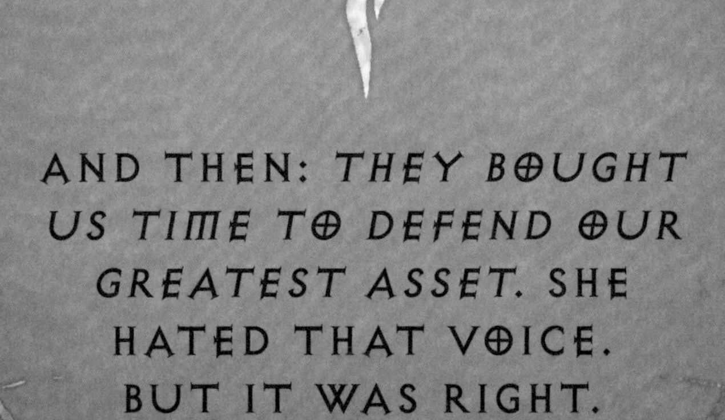

AND THEN: *THEY BOUGHT US TIME TO DEFEND OUR GREATEST ASSET.* SHE HATED THAT VOICE. BUT IT WAS RIGHT.

"Y-you can't. Help. Please."

Kez needed, more than almost anything, to look away.

"Promised." Paltik huffed the word out, wetly. *"Promised."*

She wiped her eyes. She had to focus on the battlefield.

Gart had almost no air left. Suffocating and blue-skinned, he swung his arms spasmodically, croaking at the fiends, at death itself. His words were unintelligible, save the ones Kez knew he meant for her, clear as if he had whispered them into her mind.

"No better than the sages."

It would take minutes for Paltik and Gart to die. All the while, the fiends of Mehrwen's Stay came to huddle around them in a drifting circle, easy prey for a bladedancer, even one with a broken sword. The creatures hunched down in satisfaction, their only care a chance to feed.

Kez felt a burn worse than her wounds as she held her breath and kept still, waiting for the battle's focus to shift. Waiting for her chance.

Her sword was ice cold in her hands, and the mists hugged her close.

Kynon bundled up against the wind, though the wool itched at him fiercely. Most of his retinue remained on the barge, unnerved—though they would never admit it—by the inchoate whispers that seemed to leak from the Stay's valley. Another hour and they would agitate to leave, with vague concern for *his* safety as the excuse.

A sage was the death of uncertainty. He had sent the atoners from Rag Sound to kill fiends, and he would not leave without knowledge of their success or failure. So he walked over to the valley's edge, flanked by two guards, the moment he heard the crunch of sediment beneath boots.

Kez limped from the valley and stood feet from him, unmoving. The guards drew back with their throwing spears, preparing for anything. She looked up at them, wild hair matted down by blood and rain, and her face was unearthly calm, as if it had been frozen still. Though her leathers were rent, she did not shiver, and her lips did not move. She was silent.

Kez had a bundle in her arms. Kynon gestured for the guards to hold their weapons.

He stepped forward and appraised. Gravel clung to her boots where she had walked. No hint of the mists stuck to the whites of her eyes.

Sage Kynon signaled the all clear, and the guards lowered their weapons and turned to shore. Kez walked ahead of them, saying nothing, gait steady as she neared the barge.

She was hot-blooded and arrogant, to be sure. Even after atonement. But such spirit could be tempered, even harnessed. She was also talented and cunning. A survivor.

For years, the great Unmoored, watchers of Pelghain, had warned their sages of a darkness rising to crash upon the isles. It was a danger beyond the deluge and the mists, one that threatened to unmake their home entirely. The Unmoored were no prognosticators; their shifting eyes only looked backward into history. They could not say, or did not know, what form the darkness might take. Only that it was the greatest doom of a nation born to them.

If Kez excelled as a Tempest, she could help find it, endure it—perhaps, one day, even see the dark gone, the storm halted, the empire reborn. And it would be Kynon's foresight that brought her to the capital.

"What of your atonement?" he asked when she stood a few feet from the barge. "What of the others?"

Kez unfurled the bundle she carried and let the contents clatter out onto the deck of the barge: anklets and chains, pendants and gorgets. Far more than six.

"We are all guilty," she said.

When Kez boarded, nobody stopped her.

ABOUT THE AUTHORS

Z BREWER is the *New York Times* bestselling author of the Chronicles of Vladimir Tod series, as well as eight additional books (so far). They've written more short stories than they can recall and have worked as a game dev for Poorly Timed Games as narrative lead. Their pronouns are they/them. When not making readers cry because they killed off a character they loved, Z is an anti-bullying and mental health advocate. Plus, they have awesome hair. Z lives in Buffalo, New York. They are the proud owner of a cob of human teeth. You can learn more about them at zbrewerbooks.com.

JONATHAN MABERRY is a *New York Times* bestselling author, five-time Bram Stoker Award winner, four-time Scribe Award winner, Inkpot Award winner, anthology editor, writing teacher, comic book writer, and editor of *Weird Tales* magazine. His works include the Joe Ledger thrillers *Rot & Ruin*, *Kagen the Damned*, *Ink*, *X-Files*, *V-Wars*, *Glimpse*, *Black Panther*, *Captain America*, *Wolverine*, *Punisher*, *Bad Blood*, *The Wolfman*, *Mars One*, and many others. He is the president of the International Association of Media Tie-In Writers. He lives in San Diego with his wife, Sara, and their fierce little dog, Rosie.

ALMA KATSU has been writing novels since 2011. The majority of Alma Katsu's books combine historical fiction with supernatural or horror elements. Her work has received starred reviews from *Publishers Weekly*, *Booklist*, and *Library Journal*; been featured in the *New York Times* and *Washington Post*; been nominated and won awards in the US and internationally; and appeared on numerous Best Books lists, including NPR, Apple Books, Goodreads, and Amazon. "The Hunger" (2018), a reimagining of the story of the Donner Party, was named one of NPR's 100 favorite horror stories and continues to be honored as a new classic in horror. Her most recent horror novel, *The Fervor*, has been nominated for the Stoker and Locus awards for best horror and for best hardcover by International Thriller Writers. She also writes spy thrillers, the logical marriage of her love of storytelling with her thirty-plus-year career in intelligence. *Red Widow* (2021), her first spy novel, was a *New York Times* Editor's Choice and nominated for International Thriller Writers' Best Novel. The second book in the series, *Red London*, was published March 2023 to excellent reviews and has been optioned for a TV series.

RYAN QUINN has worked for Blizzard Entertainment in communications, writing, and editing roles since 2004. He authored over a decade of Blizzard's major game announcements, sites, and apps, and has written fiction and in-game narrative for *World of Warcraft*, *Heroes of the Storm*, *StarCraft II*, and *Diablo Immortal*. Ryan is currently a senior narrative designer at Blizzard, where he crafts gloomy stories about broken people and places despite residing in perpetually sunny Southern California.

CARLY ANNE WEST is the author of several works of spooky fiction for readers of all ages, with titles including *The Murmurings* and *The Bargaining* (Simon Pulse), and the forthcoming series the Ghosts of Nameless Island (Andrews McMeel). Her works also include the Hello Neighbor series (Scholastic), based on the fan-favorite video game, as well as contributions to the *New York Times* bestselling *Five Nights at Freddy's* literary universe (Scholastic), based on the wildly popular video game of the same name. Carly holds an MFA in English and writing from Mills College and lives in Seoul, Korea, with her family.

"Witness" written by **ALMA KATSU**,
illustrated by **IGOR SIDORENKO**

"Sanctum of Bone" written by **CARLY ANNE WEST**,
illustrated by **ASHER**

"Teeth of the Plague" written by **Z BREWER**,
illustrated by **MACIEJ JANASZEK**

"The Toll of Darkness and Light" written by **JONATHAN MABERRY**,
illustrated by **YEUNJAE JANG**

"Instincts" written by **RYAN QUINN**,
illustrated by **SANGSOO JEONG**

"We Are All Guilty" written by **RYAN QUINN**,
illustrated by **CYNTHIA SHEPPARD**

EDITED BY:
CHLOE FRABONI, ERIC GERON, SYDNEY KING

ART DIRECTION BY:
COREY PETERSCHMIDT

DESIGNED BY:
JESSICA RODRIGUEZ

PRODUCED BY:
BRIANNE MESSINA, AMBER PROUE-THIBODEAU

LORE CONSULTATION BY:
MADI BUCKINGHAM, IAN LANDA-BEAVERS

GAME TEAM CONSULTATION BY:
NICK CHILANO, LEWIS HARRIS, VIVIANE KOSTY, DAVID LOMELI, JOHN MUELLER, RAFAL PRASZCZALEK, DAVID RODRIGUEZ, JOE SHELY, MAC SMITH, SEBASTIAN STEPIEN, DANIEL TANGUAY

SPECIAL THANKS:
MATTHEW BERGER, OTIS BLUM, SCOTT BURGESS, TODD CASTILLO, JUSTIN DYE, FERNANDO FORERO, QIAN LIN LIU, JESS LYTTON, JUSTIN MURRAY, EMIL SALIM, HUNTER SCHULZ, SCOTT SHICOFF, BEN WAGNER, MIKE YAKLIN, AND THE *DIABLO IMMORTAL* TEAM—PAST AND PRESENT

BLIZZARD ENTERTAINMENT

Manager, Publishing: **PETER MOLINARI**

Associate Manager, Consumer Products: **CHANEE' GOUDE**

Senior Director, Story & Franchise Development: **VENECIA DURAN**

Senior Manager, Writing & Books: **MATTHEW COHAN**

Senior Producer, Books: **BRIANNE MESSINA**

Associate Producer, Books: **AMBER PROUE-THIBODEAU**

Editorial Supervisor: **CHLOE FRABONI**

Senior Brand Artist: **COREY PETERSCHMIDT**

Associate Manager, Creative Development Production: **JAMIE ORTIZ**

Producer, Lore: **ED FOX**

Lore Historian Lead: **SEAN COPELAND**

Associate Historian: **IAN LANDA-BEAVERS**

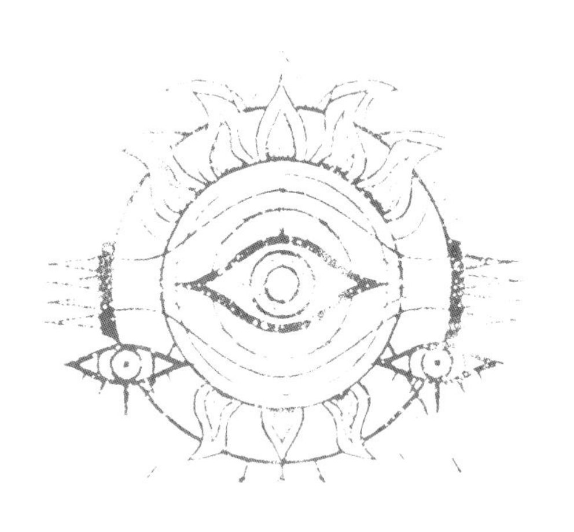